C0-ALW-090

"Put on your suit, Sasha, or I'll do it for you," Marc threatened.

He crossed the room to her and caught hold of her towel by its upper edge, drawing her toward him.

"Stop that!" she hissed.

"Stop me!" he challenged, tugging on the towel again.

"Marc," she breathed. "I said I was sorry for tripping you." He was close, so close Sasha could smell the salty musk of his skin. "What are you going to do?" she asked, as his fingers grazed her skin, thrilling her, burning her.

He laughed softly. "Somehow drowning you doesn't have the appeal it once did." His stare sent a laser of anticipation down her spine. He brushed a jeweled bead of water from her collarbone and pulled her closer, loosening the towel.

"I don't approve of this, Marc," she whispered as he caressed her throat.

Her voice had the sound of a woman who wanted to taste forbidden fruit.

"Is that why your heart's so wild?"

"I could scream—"

"You won't. You don't want to wake up from this dream any more than I do. . . ."

WHAT ARE *LOVESWEPT* ROMANCES?

They are stories of true romance and touching emotion. We believe those two very important ingredients are constants in our highly sensual and very believable stories in the *LOVESWEPT* line. Our goal is to give you, the reader, stories of consistently high quality that may sometimes make you laugh, sometimes make you cry, but are always fresh and creative and contain many delightful surprises within their pages.

Most romance fans read an enormous number of books. Those they truly love, they keep. Others may be traded with friends and soon forgotten. We hope that each *LOVESWEPT* romance will be a treasure—a "keeper." We will always try to publish

LOVE STORIES YOU'LL NEVER FORGET
BY AUTHORS YOU'LL ALWAYS REMEMBER

The Editors

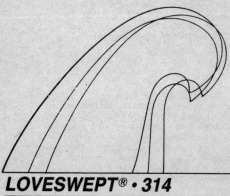

LOVESWEPT® • 314

Suzanne Forster
Wild Honey

 BANTAM BOOKS
TORONTO • NEW YORK • LONDON • SYDNEY • AUCKLAND

WILD HONEY

A Bantam Book / March 1989

*LOVESWEPT® and the wave device are registered
trademarks of Bantam Books, a division of
Bantam Doubleday Dell Publishing Group, Inc.
Registered in U.S. Patent
and Trademark Office and elsewhere.*

*All rights reserved.
Copyright © 1989 by Suzanne Forster.
Cover art copyright © 1989 by Lino Saffioti.
No part of this book may be reproduced or transmitted
in any form or by any means, electronic or mechanical,
including photocopying, recording, or by any information
storage and retrieval system, without permission in
writing from the publisher.
For information address: Bantam Books.*

*If you would be interested in receiving protective vinyl
covers for your Loveswept books, please write to this address
for information:*

Loveswept
Bantam Books
P.O. Box 985
Hicksville, NY 11802

ISBN 0-553-21971-5

Published simultaneously in the United States and Canada

Bantam Books are published by Bantam Books, a division
of Bantam Doubleday Dell Publishing Group, Inc. Its trademark, consisting of the words "Bantam Books" and the
portrayal of a rooster, is Registered in U.S. Patent and
Trademark Office and in other countries. Marca Registrada.
Bantam Books, 666 Fifth Avenue, New York, New York 10103.

PRINTED IN THE UNITED STATES OF AMERICA

O   0 9 8 7 6 5 4 3 2 1

One

It was "high noon" at eight A.M. in Sasha McCleod's tiny Redondo Beach, California, kitchen. It was Sasha's year to cut out the things that weren't working in her life, and she'd promised herself that her compulsive tidiness would be the first thing to go. Sasha McCleod was going head-to-head with her demons this fine January morning.

Her shoulders squared, she continued her stare-down with the dirty breakfast dishes she'd just put into the kitchen sink.

Messiness is not genetic, she told herself, stepping back from the sink. It can be learned. She took a long, fortifying breath. Today dirty breakfast dishes, tomorrow the top off the toothpaste, and next week, she decided recklessly, undies on the bedroom floor.

She turned away from the sink, and with a sigh of victory glanced at the framed photograph on the opposite wall. Bird Colonel Jack McCleod, U.S. Air Force, stared back at her. "No offense, sir," she said, "but there's got to be more to life than polishing doorknobs to a high gloss. I'm not lowering my standards," she explained. "I'm just re-laxing them a little."

The words were barely out of Sasha's mouth, and she felt the tug of opposing inner forces. Even at thirty she was still her father's daughter, and the urge to achieve perfection in everything was strong.

The kitchen wall phone went off like a burglar alarm, startling Sasha out of her dilemma. It rang again before she reached it. "Hello?"

"Alexandria McCleod?" a raspy male voice inquired.

"Yes," she said tentatively. In the next seconds all she could hear was the wheeze of heavy breathing. A prank call, she decided, smiling. And she knew exactly who the prankster was. Mike, her office manager at the health club, also known as Top Cat or T.C., was infamous for his practical jokes.

"Alexandria, this is Louis Ryan, your agent," the man said. "And, lady, have I got a break for you. A fabulous deal—" He broke off in a raucous fit of sneezing, interspersed with what sounded suspiciously like laughter.

Her *agent*? Now Sasha knew it was a practical joke—and not a very good one. She'd given up her acting career over a year before and hadn't heard from her theatrical agent in at least that long. She'd literally haunted Louis Ryan's office after he'd taken her on as a client. Eager to work, she'd gone out on audition after audition. But the rejections finally wore her down, especially since the casting directors' reasons were always the same. She looked too much like a famous actress. She'd had just two acting jobs in all that time, both commercials. The last one, for Yum Yum Yogurt, was a standing gag around The Fitness Factor, the small health club she owned and operated. "No Emmy nominations yet?" the staff members were fond of asking her.

"There'll be a limo to pick you up," the man added, his voice gurgling as the sneezing tapered off.

"Nice try, T.C.," Sasha murmured coolly.

"Nice what?"

"Sure, a limo," she said, "and I'll bet I won the Irish Sweepstakes too. Now, stop this foolishness, T.C. and make yourself useful. Sharpen pencils or something. I'm on my way. I'll be there in fifteen minutes."

With characteristic briskness she hung up the phone, grabbed the bulging athletic bag from a kitchen chair, and started for the front door. As her hand closed on the shiny doorknob, the phone rang again.

She turned back to it, faintly annoyed. T.C. never did know when to quit. Jogging back, she whisked the receiver up. "Okay, wise guy, what now?"

"Miss McCleod? Now, listen to me. There isn't much time. This *is* Louis Ryan of Talent International—and I've got an urgent offer—for *you*."

The athletic bag slipped from Sasha's fingers and dropped to the floor. "Oh my God . . . Lou Ryan?" she whispered. "You don't sound like Lou Ryan."

"Asthma," he said. "Who can breathe in this weather? Ninety-degree heat in January, first-stage smog alerts. The air outside my office is staring back at me! Agghh," he wheezed, "don't get me started."

"Lou, did you say . . . a fabulous deal?"

"Now she wants to talk business," he muttered.

"Yes, I said a fabulous deal. Can you make an audition today?"

"An audition?" She hardly could believe what she was hearing. "I think so. When?"

"Now. The rep of a major studio called this morning. They're sending a limo to pick you up."

Taking the receiver with her, Sasha peeked out the kitchen window and gasped. A black Cadillac limousine rivaling the length of her apartment idled in the parking lot. "It's already here! *What* studio? What's this all about?" she asked.

"Damned if I can figure it out," he admitted. "I'm not allowed to say who called or what studio he represents, but I can tell you the request is legit. They want you to audition. And if you get the job, it's big money."

He mentioned a figure that made Sasha's jaw go slack. "What do they want me for?" she asked. "A movie? Television? Why all the secrecy?"

"Slow down," he said. "I've already told you everything I *can* tell you. The studio's got a tight lid on this project. Any leaks and they come after my head. You pay me for my advice, Ms. McCleod, so I'll give you some. Go on this audition and read like you've never read before. Whoever they want you to play, play her for all you're worth. Burn up that script with your interpretation."

"But—"

"And when you're done," he added cryptically. "Say nothing, and see nothing. Know what I mean?"

"No, I don't, Lou. I don't understand at all. Say nothing? See nothing? What does that mean?"

"Sasha, it's *big* money."

He quoted the amount again, and Sasha's protests died on her lips. Her brain began clicking like an adding machine. She had a balloon payment coming up on the fitness center's second mortgage. The money from this job would cover it three times over! "Are you sure this is legit, Lou? I mean it's not X rated or anything?"

"Didn't you hear me? I said it's a *major* studio!"

"Right," she said, her heart beginning to pound. She glanced at the car again and wondered if she was dreaming. After all those months, *years* of rejection, somebody wanted her badly enough to send a limo? It made no sense.

"What's it going to be?" Lou pressed.

It wasn't like her to go into anything uninformed or ill prepared, but after all, she thought, it wasn't as if she were committing herself to anything. It was just an audition. "Okay, I'll do it. Sure," she said, laughing nervously, "I'll do it."

"Great," Lou answered. "Call me when they cut you loose. Good luck!"

Sasha hung up the phone and looked down at her outfit—turquoise leotard and tights, matching leg warmers, and running shoes. Her long blond hair was pulled back and woven into a French braid that hung down below the curve between her shoulder blades. She wore no makeup except a bit of blusher, mascara, and lip gloss.

The doorbell rang as she was fishing for her jeans in the athletic bag. Her heart sank. There was no time to change. She would have to go as she was. A leotard to an audition? A sinkful of breakfast dishes? she thought. "Someone up there is testing me," she said on a sigh. It was more than any perfectionist should be expected to deal with in one day.

The doorbell rang again more insistently as Sasha walked to the door and swung it open. She smiled politely at a man with a pale, pencil-thin face, which was lost behind a huge pair of wrap-around sunglasses. "Hello," she said, sizing him up instantly as posing no threat. His uniform bagged over a bony frame not much taller than her own five feet eight inches.

Minutes later, headed for an unspecified location, surrounded by windows as opaque as the driver's glasses, Sasha began to question the wisdom of her decision. Another twenty minutes passed, and her doubts mushroomed. What could she have been thinking about when she got into the sleek black motel of a car? She had no idea where the driver was taking her, who wanted to audition her—or even if it really had been Lou Ryan on the phone.

The window that separated her from the driver was opaque, too, and tapping on it raised no response. She told herself not to panic, but a sudden claustrophobic wave of heat stirred her nerves and her imagination. She'd been kidnapped. Her abductors were going to sell her to swarthy men who hid switchblades in their boots.

"Whoa," she murmured, settling back in the seat, "you're a shade mature for the white slave market." Nevertheless, in the next moments her fertile imagination had her vividly displayed in a bazaar in some exotic port, a shivering nymph on an auction block with a cloaked marauder tweaking off veils one by one to drive the bidding higher. . . .

Sasha swayed with the movement of the car and caught herself. Adrift in escalating scenarios of abduction and seduction, she'd lost track of time, but suddenly she realized the limo was finally slowing, pulling over. Maybe she could persuade them to release her if she told them she was thirty and had an appendectomy scar.

By the time the driver opened her door, she'd cooled her imagination. "Take the stage door," he said, helping her out. "You'll find some stairs and a hallway to the auditorium. Wait on the stage. You'll be told what to do."

Sasha looked up and down the alley where they were parked and guessed the area to be somewhere in West L.A. From what she could discern from the building, which looked deserted, it was probably an old repertory theater. "Do you know what this is all about?" she asked the driver, virtually certain he wouldn't tell her even if he did.

He shrugged and jerked his head toward the stage door.

"Right," she said.

The stage door creaked mournfully as she opened it. The hallway was as dark and musty as a root cellar, and each creaky stair step sagged with her weight. Sasha's fears resurfaced. Tight lid or not, a major movie studio wouldn't resort to auditions in a place like this, she realized. She hesitated at the top of the stairs, her eyes following a dark, serpentine corridor. Halfway down on the left, a faint glow of light beckoned her toward the stage.

Sasha felt her pulse quicken. She gave herself a quick once-over, tugged at her leotard, smoothing its lines. Mixed with the fear was another emotion she hadn't even been aware of. Hope. She wanted this to be a legitimate audition. *She wanted this part no matter what it turned out to be*—and not just for the money. In her heart of hearts she had always wanted to be an actress.

Sasha ran her fingers along the fragile gold chain around her neck, touched the antique charm, and drew strength from it. It was the one remembrance she had of her long-absent mother, the Russian Gypsy who'd deserted her husband and her six-year-old daughter a quarter century before. Alexandria. The woman she was named for.

The stage was dark except for a single stool flooded by a spotlight. Squinting at the brightness, she couldn't move for a minute, might not have moved at all if the pull of the floodlit stool hadn't been so great. Walking toward it through the darkness, she felt like an orbiting body being tugged toward the sun's critical mass.

Despite the nerve-sparked trembling inside her, she arranged herself on the high seat gracefully, looked up, and smiled. Blinded by the spotlight for a second, she could see nothing beyond the white wall of light that enveloped her.

A shuffle of movement alerted her, the clink of something metal. Someone was in the auditorium.

A spark caught her eye. The striking of a match, she realized, watching the disembodied flame ignite tiny red embers before it disappeared. Now she knew something more than she had before. Her inquisitor smoked.

"Tell me about yourself, Ms. McCleod."

Sasha started as though someone had touched her. Transfixed by the flickering ember of the cigarette, her brain registered several more bits of information. Her inquisitor was male. His voice was low and resonant, faintly laced with European inflections. And his voice was cold, crushed-ice cold.

"I've done a variety of things, a commercial—"

"I know what you've done," he said, cutting her off. "I want to know about *you*, not your professional credits. Tell me about yourself."

Staring into the black hole of an auditorium, Sasha wrestled with the enormity of his question. Tell him about herself? Did he want a life history? A brief personal profile? If he'd meant to throw her a curve, he had. "I'm a thirty-year-old actress who wants to know what the hell's going on," she said finally, quietly.

The cigarette froze, a still beacon in the darkness.

Her agent's advice rushed to mind. *Ask no questions, say nothing, see nothing.* When would she learn to play the game? Her tendency toward confrontational honesty had been getting her into trouble since the day she'd first learned to string a sentence together.

"Sorry, but I'm not free to tell you what the hell's going on," he said, a husky hint of spring thaw in his voice. "With that in mind, do you want to continue the audition?"

"Yes."

"Good. Then tell me what I need to know about Sasha McCleod."

His voice did things to her name that had never been done before. The lingering emphasis on the last syllable of Sasha, and the sensual roll of the vowels in McCleod felt almost tactile. Without warning, the fine blond hairs on Sasha's arms prickled, and her breathing quivered slightly. She wasn't at all sure she wanted someone getting so familiar with her name.

"I'm an air force brat," she said, the odd rush in her voice somehow glamorizing her hopelessly unglamorous history. "I was born in Albuquerque, on the base, of course. By the time I was ready to enter school, I guess I'd lived on half the air force bases in the country." She chronicled the rest of her past briefly, told him about the fitness center and her acting experience, which she had the presence of mind to embellish with a couple of funny stories. Her energy rose as she talked, and with it, her desire to make an impression on him. Yes, she did want the part, she decided.

Wondering about the silent figure she was pouring out her heart to, Sasha found herself predicting his reactions by the movements of his cigarette. When it was motionless, she figured she had his attention.

"I studied with the Brownings," she finished up, smiling. "Rowen and Anna. They're very eclectic in their approach—Stanislavsky, Method, some of the other experiential techniques. I particularly liked their Gestalt workshops."

The red embers glowed hotter, then dipped impatiently. "What *don't* you like, Sasha?"

"What don't I li—" The question stopped her for only a moment. Sasha was passionate in her dislikes, something of a crusader, in fact. "Well, I can't abide conceit of any kind, I get homicidal when people cut in front of me in traffic, and I've been known to pluck cigarettes out of people's mouths and snap them in half."

The embers hung in the air.

"For . . . health reasons, of course." Struck with the awareness of what she'd said, she added, "One man even thanked me. He said I saved his life." Her conviction grew fainter with each word. "I still hear from him occasionally . . . every November twentieth on Great American Smokeout Day."

The embers vanished altogether, crushed into oblivion on the auditorium floor, no doubt. Sasha shifted uncomfortably and began to memorize the cracks in the stage floor.

From his seat in the depths of the auditorium, Marc-André Renaud smiled faintly as he ground out a Gauloise under the heel of his boot. His interest piqued, he leaned forward, studying the woman on the stage as she flicked her head, a nervous gesture meant to toss the stray blond tendrils from her face. Despite the nerves, there was a natural grace in the way she held herself, in her sloped shoulders, in the arch of her throat. She was lovely, he admitted reluctantly, she was glowing and golden, with the toned body and vital, healthy presence of a superior athlete.

His pulse jumped as she looked up, straight at him, peering into the darkness as though she could see him. He knew she couldn't, but he had the most uncanny sensation of having been caught at something. His heart was beating harder, and the possibility that she could have such an effect on him, that *anyone* could have such an effect on him, was curious in itself.

He settled back in the chair, cutting off the response quickly, efficiently, with a simple flex of his steel willpower. The momentary lapse had been almost pleasant, but he needed his wits about him today. There could be no slipups, no mistakes. The only thing that mattered, he reminded himself, was Sasha McCleod's resemblance to Leslie Parrish. And the fact that the studio's production chief would be arriving at any minute to hear his decision.

Up on the stage the woman in question took a long breath and tucked her leg beneath her, obviously nervous. A production assistant was hovering in the background with the script. "Give her the pages, Jimmy," Marc directed.

"Right," Jimmy called back.

Startled, Sasha jerked around and saw a young man approaching her from the wings. She felt the unsteadiness in her own hands as he handed her a worn, marked-up script which she might have dropped if he hadn't tucked it so firmly into her grip. "Thank you," she whispered.

"Relax," he said under his breath, a friendly swagger in his voice. "You're a sure thing. You could be her twin sis—"

"*Jimmy!* One more slip like that," the disembodied voice warned harshly, "and you're off this picture. Now, clear out."

"Was that necessary?" she demanded.

"Turn to page thirty-two and read, Ms. McCleod. Or you'll be the next to leave."

Sasha snapped through the pages, found the one he wanted, and began reading. Her voice tight, her spine stiff, she massacred lines that called for a halting, tearful reconciliation with a loved one. "I'm no good without you, Charlie," she said. "I've been crazy with loneliness, Charlie, wild with needing you . . ."

Aware that she was killing whatever chance she had left, Sasha also became aware of something else. Above the sound of her own voice she heard the rustle of feet and the low tones of conversation. There was more than one person in the auditorium.

"Thank you. That'll do," a second male voice called out just as Sasha was reminding herself that large amounts of money and a fabulous deal were at stake. Again, Lou Ryan's words came to her seconds too late. *Burn up that script with your interpretation.*

"Excuse me? Sir?" she asked, squinting into the darkness. "I was just getting into the scene, just beginning to feel its rhythms—" She held up the book. "If I could try it again?" Hearing mumbled conversation resume, she flipped back to the first page. "Charlie, oh, *Charlie*," she read, her voice soaked with emotion. "I'm no good without you. I—"

"Nice," he called out. "Really, very nice, Ms.

McCleod, but we've heard enough. There's a dressing room backstage. If you'll wait there, someone will be with you in a minute."

The dressing room was a peeling mess of warped and water-stained plasterboard. Seated on a wobbly folding chair, Sasha contemplated her dismal surroundings. She held out no hope for the role, and as the minutes ticked off, she began to wonder if she'd been forgotten by the limo driver too. The man in the theater had said he'd send someone by for her. Where was he?

A half hour later she was pacing nervously. Perhaps she'd just leave the way she came in, find a phone booth, and call a taxi.

Staring at a gruesome crack in the ceiling, her fingers splayed against her face, Sasha heard the door open behind her. "Oh, thank God," she said, whirling around, totally unprepared for the sight of the man who entered the room.

Swaying slightly with the unspent momentum of her turn, she stared at him like a starstruck autograph-seeker, sure that tall and devastatingly handsome as he was, he must be some kind of movie star.

Ironically Sasha didn't care much for actors, especially tall and devastatingly handsome actors. But this one had eyes like ice crystals backlit by a sheer blue sky. His dark eyebrows accented the coldest, palest gaze she'd ever seen. His hair was dark, too, a devil's aura, and the sensual twist to his full mouth stirred Sasha's imagination . . . and her heartbeat.

It was a mouth a woman couldn't look at without wondering what it would feel like on hers. It was a face of startling shadings and cruel contrasts. And Sasha McCleod, a woman not easily awed, was riveted.

"The Brownings couldn't have been much good," he said, "or they would have prepared you for cold readings."

So this was her inquisitor, she realized.

"The Brownings are geniuses, both of them," she said. "The reading was my fault. I was . . . upset."

He shifted his weight, cocked his head slightly, studying her. "And this is your style, to be upset?"

If the year were 1945, he could be a World War II resistance fighter, she thought, reacting to the image that flashed through her mind. A *French* resistance fighter. He had on worn jeans, a black turtleneck that electrified the ice blue of his eyes, and a battered leather bomber jacket. A vague recollection burned through Sasha's vision. No, he wasn't a movie star or a reincarnated resistance fighter, but she had seen him before . . . somewhere.

"Turn your head to the right," he said, his thumb pressed against his lower lip thoughtfully.

She did it automatically, but a cord within her tightened. Sasha harbored a fierce dislike of anything resembling an order. After a lifetime of the colonel's benign authoritarianism, she'd nurtured a grudging respect for, and a smoldering resentment of authority.

"A determined chin," he observed, his voice detached but not exactly indifferent. "Now the left."

She resisted instinctively, met his wintry stare, and turned her head to the left. "What's this all about," she asked. "Why am I here?"

"Look at me now, yes, smile at me," he said, ignoring her questions. "A *smile*," he directed quietly, "not a death grimace. You have a good mouth, nicely shaped. Yes, *yes*, that's it, a smile. Now take a full turn and walk away from me."

Turning, Sasha realized she didn't like the man's methods. Good mouth indeed. He was manipulating her, conning her like some gullible, simpering actress. Beyond that he was several notches too cool. Self-assured was the word that came to mine—ruthlessly self-assured.

"Turn back. Stop, stop there." His eyes flashed like sunlight bouncing off glass. "Now . . . untie that thing."

"What?" Sasha's fingers froze on the zippered bodice of her leotard. "Why?"

"It's a sexy picture." He shrugged, folded his arms. "I need a sexy actress."

A nerve sparked in Sasha's hand. She felt her heart pounding, felt heat crawling up her neck. He'd caught her off guard, and it wasn't just his request that alarmed her. She'd suddenly remembered who he was. Marc-André Renaud, the expatriate French film director the entertainment columnists were fond of bashing. They'd labeled him autocratic and difficult. If she remembered correctly, he'd hit a studio vice-president two years before and had been blacklisted.

He was infamous for other things as well, she recalled, such as his scorchingly sensual *film noir* style.

The plastic zipper tab of the leotard cut into the soft flesh of Sasha's thumb and forefinger. Her heart hammering, she lowered it fractionally and stopped as something took shape inside her, a tightening spiral of anxiety. It radiated into her belly, oddly exciting, wholly disturbing. She parted her lips, wetting their sudden dryness with a nervous dart of her tongue. With a shallow breath she lowered the zipper another inch and then her fingers locked, frozen stiff by the sensations inside her.

He exhaled, his thumb working at his lower lip. "The idea of a sensual role frightens you, doesn't it?" he said quietly.

Sasha might have admitted the truth to anyone else but not to him. Her intuition was flooding her with signals, the strongest of which was that he already had decided against her for the part, whatever it was. Some sixth sense told her that he was testing her, pushing her to her limits, looking for a reason to reject her. The realization stirred her courage. "I'm an actress," she said, her voice faint but firm. "And I'm not afraid of sensuality. If a role calls for it, I can be sexy. Believe it."

The only movement in the room was the blink of his eyes. Energy moved in their blue depths, mesmerizing energy.

Sasha took a quick breath, and in the glance that passed between them, something unexpected happened, an unchecked impulse, quick and electric. She felt it like a hot wire to her nerves. Then her heart became a slow fuse, showering sparks, threatening to go off like a Fourth of July rocket. Stunned, she took a half step back.

Marc felt the impulse too. It ran like a current through his muscles.

Before either of them could speak, the door opened and a tall, graying man, trim in a navy blazer, walked into the room. He clapped Marc on the back in the jovial, placating gesture of a man who wanted everything to run smoothly. His gaze on Sasha, he spoke to Marc. "Well, what do you think? Will she work?"

Sasha's heart jerked as Marc looked at her. Apparently everything hinged on Marc's opinion, and she found herself hoping, however foolishly, that she *would* work in Marc Renaud's judgment.

"Sorry, Paul," he said to the studio's head of production. "She's a couple inches too tall. And she can't take direction."

Paul's face fell. "The height can be hidden."

Sasha's first reaction was sharp disappointment. Her second was indignation. *Can't take direction?* She drew the zipper of her leotard down several inches and pulled the ribbon from her braid. Combing her fingers into her hair, she loosened the plaits, shaking her head until a dazzling fall of white-gold hair shimmered around her face. "You wanted sexy, Mr. Renaud?" Tossing her head back, she drew herself up and met Marc's gaze. Her mouth twitched with a devastating smile.

Paul's jaw went slack. "Marc, what's wrong with you? She's fabulous."

Stepping back, Marc acknowledged the golden firestorm of Sasha McCleod's cascading hair. He knew unfettered loveliness when he saw it—and he knew trouble. *Take me on, Mr. Renaud,* her eyes seemed to say, *if you're up to the challenge.* His blood stirring, he watched her amber irises become almost black . . . and felt his heartbeat accelerate. He'd almost forgotten the rush of excitement that came from dealing with someone like her, someone strong enough to challenge him.

He scrutinized her carefully. Physically she was extraordinary, close to a perfect match, but it would be insanity to risk her on this picture, and he knew it. There was too much at stake. She was strong-willed, and his intuition told him she'd fight him every inch of the way. No, he couldn't risk it.

As he turned to an eager Paul Maxwell with the bad news, his final thought was of her eyes, the rich amber color of the wild honey he used to buy from the peasant farmers in l'Auvergne. Honey so drizzly warm, so sweet that the first taste always made his jaws ache.

"What do you say, Marc?" Paul Maxwell prodded.

Marc gestured toward the door. Drawing Paul with him into the murky hallway, he shook his head. "She's not right."

"But Marc—"

His self-control reasserted itself, icing his voice. "I *said* she's not right. Tell them they'll have to get me someone else."

Two

Torturous groans rocked The Fitness Factor's gymnasium.

"Have mercy," someone said weakly. "That's *fifty*."

"No more!" another pleaded.

"Ten situps to go," Sasha called out from her pad at the head of the health club's early-bird exercise class. "On the count. Altogether now. One—up! Two-up!"

With each command, forty straining, sweating bodies wrenched themselves up from supine positions and touched their elbows to their bent knees. "Uncle, uncle," someone screamed.

Sasha gritted her teeth, her stomach muscles burning with each effort. "Three—up! Come on, you pansies," she said with a groan, "hustle the muscle! Four—up! Five—up!"

"What'd she have for breakfast? Steroids?" a breathless woman complained.

"Either that or she's working off a truckload of frustration," another said.

Give that lady a gold star, Sasha thought.

"Six—up! Seven . . ." She grimaced as she routed the last trace of anger from her system. Exercise was the way Sasha McCleod purged her wrath, and the cavalier treatment she'd received at the audition the day before had generated some serious wrath. *Not right for the part, my fanny!* she thought indignantly. "Eight—up! Nine," she counted. Paul Maxwell had tried to let her down gently, and even though he'd been the hatchet man, she knew it wasn't he who'd cost her the job. It had been that blue-eyed ice cube of a Frenchman. Anger built anew. "Ten more!"

"No way!" a chorus of voices protested.

"Ease up, boss," her office manager's voice called from the gym doorway. "You're killing off the clientele."

"Okay," Sasha agreed. Dropping to the floor, she stretched out, her arms limp, her legs spread-eagled. "Okay, you pansies, fall out for a cool-down. Don't forget good deep breathing now."

A collective moan of relief went up as bodies dropped one by one, to the gymnasium floor.

Too weak to move, Sasha heard a familiar swoosh of movement coming toward her, then a low chuckle.

"You're beautiful when you're wet, boss."

Even with her eyes closed she could visualize her office manager's irrepressible grin. "A little respect, T.C.," she murmured. "Especially if you're about to hit me up for a raise again."

The rubbery squeak and screech of wheels against the hard wood floor brought her eyes open fast. Jockeying his shiny chrome wheelchair like a customized dirt bike, T.C. spun out a 360-degree turn right in front of her eyes, ending the spin with the front wheels teetering precariously in the air at a heart-stopping 45-degree angle.

Sasha propped up on one elbow. It was a performance she'd seen many times since T.C.'s skiing accident the year before, but it never failed to take her breath away with its stark proof of heart and mind over matter. T.C. had lost the use of his legs but not his will to soar with eagles. "I'm heading back to the office," he told Sasha. "Need a lift?"

She shook her head. "I could use a heart monitor and some oxygen if you have any handy."

He stared down at her spent body, wisdom in his young twenty-two-year-old features. "Trust me, you need a lift." Anchoring his chair wheel with one hand, he held out the other to her. "On your feet, boss lady."

Sasha took his hand. "Whoops!" she cried, half laughing, half groaning as he snapped her upright, twirled her around, and dropped her onto his lap.

The women in the exercise class managed a couple of "attaboys" and some weak applause as T.C. wheeled his chair around and headed for the hallway to the health club's office.

"No speeding and *no wheelies*," Sasha said, hanging onto his neck as he negotiated the door and made a smooth right turn. "I got motion sickness the last time you gave me a lift."

"No wheelies," he promised, "but you're seriously cramping my style. I can lay rubber with this baby."

Sasha believed him. So far there didn't seem to be anything T.C. couldn't do with his wheels. "I'm waiting for the tightrope act," she told him dryly.

As they rolled down the tiled hallway, T.C. seemingly resigned to safe and sane driving, Sasha relaxed a little.

She was jarred back into awareness as T.C.

accelerated toward the ramp that led to the business office downstairs.

"If you're thinking about burning rubber down that ramp, think again," she warned him, pulling his surfer's T-shirt out of shape with her nervous grip.

"Burn rubber?" He chuckled dangerously. "Hell, I'm not even going to take the ramp."

He cornered a sharp turn and stopped inches from the top of the stairway next to the ramp. "Hold tight, boss."

Sasha glanced down the short flight of stairs and back at T.C., her eyes widening as she realized what he was about to do. "Oh, my God, T.C.! Don't take the stairw—wah—wah—wah—wah—*waaaay*!" she wailed as they bounced all the way down, hit the landing, and skidded across the corridor into the office.

When he finally came to a gliding stop next to the desk, she had her head tucked into the curve of his shoulder, her eyes squeezed shut. "Did we make it?" she asked, feeling for her pulse. "I think my heart has stopped."

Grinning, T.C. pressed his fingertips to the throbbing artery in her neck. "Took a lickin', but you're still tickin'." He helped her out of the chair and steadied her until she had her balance.

"Someday, T.C.," she promised ominously, straightening her leotard and pulling up her leg warmers, "you'll give the wrong person a ride on that thing—a hijacker, I hope—and you'll end up in Cuba."

Helping her rearrange the leg warmers, he smiled up at her. "Scared you, huh? Sorry."

"Don't try to make up," she said, fighting back an answering grin. "You're not a bit sorry."

The phone rang, cutting off his protestations of remorse. As he wheeled past her to the desk to answer it, she swiped his towel and held it up to her heated face and neck. The paperwork could wait. What she needed was a tall, icy glass of carrot juice and a soak in the Jacuzzi.

She was on her way out the door when she heard T.C. say, "Yeah, she's here. Paul who?"

She halted midstride, her heart galloping. Don't be ridiculous, she told herself. There's a better chance that it's the apostle from the Bible than Paul Maxwell, the production chief she'd met the day before.

Still, she couldn't move.

"Yo! Sasha!" T.C. called. "Paul Maxwell."

She whirled around. Her feet seemed to move independently of the rest of her as she scrambled back into the office, took the phone receiver from T.C., and caught herself. Holding the phone against her chest, she said, "Steady, girl."

"What's going on?" T.C. asked, watching her.

She shushed him, counted to ten silently, and put the phone to her ear. "Mr. Maxwell?"

"Sasha," he said as warmly as though they were long-lost friends. "How are you?"

"Fine." She held the towel to her flushed brow. "Couldn't be better."

"Wonderful, glad to hear it. Forgive me if I get right to the point, Sasha, but I'm afraid I need to talk to you as soon as possible. I've got—well, let's call it an interesting proposition for you. How does one o'clock in my office in Century City sound?"

She grabbed T.C.'s wrist and looked at his watch. "One would be fine."

"Great, just great," Maxwell replied. He engaged her in another moment or two of cordial conversation—of which Sasha registered not one word—before he signed off with a pleasant good-bye.

Not quite sure what to do with the phone, Sasha handed it to T.C.

"Paul Maxwell must be somebody important," he said, letting the receiver drop into the cradle with a clunk. "I haven't seen you this spacey since that time lightning struck the swimming pool when you were doing your laps."

"Yes, he is important, T.C." she said absently, turning to stare out the office's one window. "And what's more, I have the strangest feeling that my meeting with him this afternoon could be the start of something . . ."

"*Big*," T.C. added.

Sasha turned, laughed . . . and felt the oddest shiver run down her spine.

Paul Maxwell's office was a tour de force in the blending of modern form and functional space. From the panoramic view of the L.A. skyline to the pale pastel modular furniture and acrylic accent pieces, it rivaled a science fiction movie for futuristic panache.

Sasha discreetly assessed her surroundings while Paul Maxwell concluded some business with his secretary. After his phone call that morning, she'd done some fast catching up on the industry in the Hollywood trade papers. She knew Gemini Pictures was considered the hot new studio in a town where "hot" and "new" were magic words. She also knew they'd had an unprecedented string of hits over the past year, each one "box office gold" according to the papers.

As the secretary left, Paul considered Sasha with

a warm smile. Returning his smile, she considered him back. He didn't look like a man "crumbling under the pressure of multimillion-dollar deals" as the trade papers had characterized the typical studio production chief.

"May I get you a drink?" he inquired, touching a button on his desk. On the opposite wall, an impressionistic mural rose to reveal an amply-stocked wet bar.

Glancing down at her clasped hands, her fingers a bloodless white at the joints, Sasha realized she was more nervous than she cared to admit. "No, I guess not," she said as he started for the bar.

He fixed himself a vodka on the rocks, took a sip as though to test his bartending skills, and splashed in some more vodka. "I met with the studio's president after the audition yesterday, Sasha," he said, turning back to her. "I showed him the videotape of the commercial your agent sent us. Afterward he was as convinced as I am that you're the actress we need for this picture. So"—He fingered the rim of the glass—"we're overruling Marc."

"I see," Sasha said, her voice betraying none of her incredulity and confusion. They'd overruled the picture's director because of her yogurt commercial?

"The things you did for that Ferrari," he was saying. "Well, I almost went out and bought one."

Now she *did* see. Several years earlier a foreign-car importer had hired her for a local spot. Looking sultry in black sequins, she'd draped herself across the wine-red Ferrari. "I don't come with the car," she'd almost purred into the camera, "but if you've got the wherewithal to buy it out from under me, I might be interested."

"A very provocative thirty seconds," Maxwell concluded.

"Thank you." Sasha managed a smile. "Does Mr. Renaud know?"

Drink in hand, he walked to a lighted glass cabinet that held plaques and statuettes, including two Oscars. Gazing at the awards, he said without the slightest hesitation, "I'm going to have to trust you with some closely guarded production secrets, Sasha. Gemini is in deep water right now. We're losing tens of thousands of dollars every day on *Tell Me No Lies*, Marc's picture."

Sasha fished for something meaningful to say and came up with an empty hook. "Really?"

He turned around, shrugged. "You must have read the gossip columns. They're already speculating that the movie is in trouble."

"And this time they're right?"

"Our star is . . . indisposed." He took a drink, holding the liquor in his mouth for a moment before swallowing. "The picture is three quarters completed, so it's too late to bring in another name, and we can't hold up production any longer."

The intercom on his phone buzzed. Ignoring it, he stirred his drink with his finger and then looked up. "That's where you come in. You not only look like her, you're athletic enough to handle the scenes that still have to be shot. Most of them are action shots, not dangerous, but since Leslie isn't 'physical,' we'd be bringing someone in anyway. . . ."

Leslie. Immediately Sasha understood. She was replacing Leslie Parrish. She almost laughed aloud. If it wasn't one of life's absurdities, then what was? How many movie and television parts had she lost because of her resemblance to Leslie Parrish? She'd given up acting once because of Leslie

Parrish! Then her agent had sent her out to test for the Ferrari commercial. Ironically the resemblance had worked in her favor there.

"There'll be other scenes, of course," Maxwell told her. "Some are tricky, but they can be faked with camera angles, lighting, voice dubbing. If it's handled right, no one should be able to tell."

"Do you mean . . . ?" Stunned, she murmured, "You want them to think I'm Leslie?"

"Sasha, they *have* to think you're Leslie."

"Why?"

He shook his head. "I'm not free to give you the details, but it has to do with the picture's financing. There are millions already invested, most of it foreign money. There are legal things, contractual things . . ."

The astonishment must have shown in Sasha's face.

Maxwell hesitated, returned to his desk. "Unfortunately we can't give you acting credit, but the money should, well—it should help compensate." He mentioned a figure even more staggering than the one Lou Ryan had dangled in front of her like a carrot. Obviously her worth had gone up overnight.

"And, naturally," he added, "Gemini Pictures wouldn't forget the actress who bailed them out of this mess."

Sasha's mouth was dry as dust. She wet her lips imperceptibly.

Maxwell nodded as though she'd agreed, and went on. "It shouldn't take more than three weeks to wrap things up. During that time we'll need your complete cooperation."

"Complete cooperation?"

"Yes, there are some conditions attached to this deal."

The intercom buzzed again, three short bursts that were impossible to ignore. Maxwell hit a button on the phone. "What is it?"

"Mr. Renaud's here, sir. He's—"

"Tell him I'm in conference. I'll—"

Paul Maxwell swallowed the last word as his office door swung open. Marc Renaud stood on the threshold. Toweringly tall and broodingly graceful, he looked for all the world like the Prince of Darkness come to claim a sinner.

"How is it I wasn't invited to this meeting, Paul?" he asked.

Sasha consulted her tangled hands. There was a dizzying undercurrent of power in Marc Renaud's question.

Paul picked up his drink, gulped it down.

Lord, was Marc about to find out he'd been overruled, Sasha wondered. If he was, she didn't want to be in the room, in the building, or even on the planet when it happened.

"I left a message, Marc," Paul said, regaining a measure of his composure. "You weren't in." He stood up, his voice taking on the soothing tones he must have cultivated in years of dealing with difficult personalities. "Why don't you come in, shut the door."

Marc did so, ignoring the chair Paul offered and sitting on the window ledge instead, his arms folded. "I take it Ms. McCleod's going to be in the picture after all? Am I right, Paul?"

At Paul's nod, Marc's features took on a stillness that left Sasha immobilized in her chair waiting for the lightning to strike. Even to breathe normally seemed dangerous in the charged atmosphere.

The silence expanded, and Sasha became aware

of the perspiration beading on Paul Maxwell's upper lip. It was beginning to look as though he had the most to lose in this confrontation, she thought, glancing from one man to the other. Especially if Renaud chose to walk out on him. An overbudget picture minus its celebrated star *and* director could become a very heavy albatross around a movie studio executive's neck.

Marc ended the confrontation with a barely perceptible nod. Paul relaxed.

"How about a drink, Marc?" he offered amiably.

It was a moment before Sasha realized that the hostilities actually were over. She'd expected nothing less than a verbal fight, maybe even a physical one. There was more going on than met the eye, she decided, observing the warning signals that passed between the two men. If she was correct, there were hidden agendas at work in this room, things she knew nothing about.

Marc took a raincheck on the drink, and the tension in Sasha's muscles began to ebb. She even unclasped her numbed fingers.

Directing his stare at her, Marc seemed quieter somehow, if not benign, then a shade less angry. "Has Paul told you the conditions yet, Ms. McCleod?" he asked.

"He was about to when you . . . arrived." The word that had come to Sasha's mind was *interrupted*, and all three of them knew it.

Marc's mouth promised a smile that he never quite delivered. Oddly, his eyes seemed to take on light and clarity as he gazed at her, as though he were drawing energy from the blue sky that framed him in the window.

"In that case, let me do the honors, Paul," he said, his gaze remaining on Sasha. "Ms. McCleod should know what she's getting into."

Sasha already had a pretty good idea what she was getting into. Marc Renaud intimidated her on every level, from his self-possession to his riveting good looks. Dealing with him would be like walking through a field of land mines blindfolded. He frightened her, and that was the problem, of course. But Sasha had been conditioned from childhood *never* to run from her fears.

"First of all," Marc started, "you're not going to be able to talk about what you're doing *to anyone*. Not even family and friends."

"Marc, don't make it sound so sinister," Paul interrupted. "Sasha," he explained with a shrug and smile, "if it gets out that Leslie's been replaced, it could have an unfortunate effect at the box office."

"A disastrous effect," Marc amended.

"I can't tell anyone?" she questioned. "For how long?"

"Hard to say," Marc cut in before Paul could answer. "The way it looks now, we're going to have to keep the lid on indefinitely."

"A month at most," Paul reassured her. "We should be able to wrap up production in two to three weeks, and we've got a wide release planned. If we can grab a big share of the box offices and hang on to it for awhile, we'll recoup our investment, maybe even pull in a profit."

Sasha knew what was going on and so did Paul Maxwell. Marc was painting a worst-case scenario, hoping to scare her off. She felt inner resources mobilizing, a prickle of heat along her neck. Aware that she would have to rearrange her entire life for the next month, and without the faintest idea how she would do it, she said, "A month doesn't sound like an unreasonable length of time, under the circumstances."

Paul Maxwell beamed. "You'll do it, then?"

She curbed the impulse to say exactly what she knew Marc didn't want her to say. "I'd like some time to think about it."

"Gemini's all out of time," Marc informed her flatly. "And you haven't heard all the conditions yet."

The undercurrents were there again, in his voice, low, powerful.

"For the period of time the film's in production," Marc informed her, "it will be necessary for you to stay in the Malibu beach house where Leslie was staying."

"Live there?"

"Yes."

"With Leslie?"

Paul jumped in. "No, Leslie's . . . away. Of course, we need to keep that fact quiet too." He smiled wanly. "We've already got a gag order on the crew—no press, no publicity. But if the paparazzi get itchy and start snapping telephoto shots, we want them to think they're snapping Leslie. We've also arranged for a car to take you to the set and back. Other than that, of course, you'll stay in seclusion at the beach house."

Sasha looked from one man to the other. "But I can't do that. I own and operate a health club."

"You have a manager," Maxwell observed.

His statement came as a shock until she realized they must have investigated her thoroughly before they'd even considered her for the job. "Yes, but he's never run the place on his own." She cringed to think of the condition of The Fitness Factor after three weeks in T.C.'s hands.

"We'll send someone to help him," Maxwell said.

"You will?" It was becoming apparent that there

wasn't much of anything Paul Maxwell wouldn't do to get her to take this job.

Marc stood. "Paul seems to have forgotten the last condition, Sasha."

He was doing it again, caressing her name with sibilant esses and half-whispered vowels. "Another condition? And what would that be?"

"Me. I live there too."

"You?"

Marc merely smiled.

Paul Maxwell sprang up to explain. "Marc and Leslie had a widely publicized relationship, Sasha. And even though their relationship is over, and has been for quite a while, Marc has continued to live at the beach house—for the sake of the project. There would be talk if he moved out of the house now. Talk of the kind we can't afford . . ."

As Paul rattled on desperately, Sasha sat back, her thoughts floundering in the quagmire of her emotions. Live in the same house with Marc Renaud? She couldn't have explained exactly why she knew such close proximity with him spelled disaster, but her foreboding was as powerful as a telepathic flashcube pop.

At last she looked up. Marc's confident expression, the glint of light hidden in his cool gaze, tipped her off to the truth. He had just played his ace. *He thinks he's won,* she realized. *He thinks he has exactly what he wants—me, out of his picture.*

Don't be so sure, her eyes told him. *Don't ever assume you can be that sure of me, mister.* She turned to Paul Maxwell. "I really will need time to think this over."

"Of course," Paul agreed.

Marc glanced at his watch. "Ten hours, Sasha. I want your answer by midnight tonight."

"Marc—" Paul protested.

Marc gave him a stony stare. "Another day, another five-figure loss, Paul. It's your money."

"Midnight's fine," Sasha said.

Turning back to her, Marc let his gaze drift over her features and brush her shoulders and breasts. "I'm sure you'll make the right decision."

She stared back at him, her heart pounding with a sudden flash of heat. She could feel the color in her cheeks, and she damn well hoped he knew it was indignation. Arrogant as he was, he probably thought she was aroused.

Marc backed to the door, nodded to her, a touch of irony in his smile. "Midnight," he said, and left.

Fixated on the door, she looked up as Paul walked around to where she sat. "Marc does take a little getting used to," he said, sitting on the edge of his desk. "But then, brilliance always brings some baggage with it, doesn't it?"

Without waiting for Sasha to comment, he walked to the awards case and tapped the beveled glass door. "Gemini has two Best Picture Oscars, Sasha. In his heyday, barely into his thirties, Marc Renaud won them both for us." Swinging around, he focused on her. "He's been making independent films since then, small masterpieces really. *Tell Me No Lies* is his comeback picture, and we want him to blow the skeptics away."

Sasha had read everything that Paul was telling her in the trades, but hearing him say it, hearing the odd note that crept into his voice . . .

"If there's any chance you're thinking of turning us down," he said, "then let me dissuade you. Marc Renaud is no ordinary moviemaker. He's a visionary, a man with a magnificent obsession, even the critics admit that. His films shatter the status quo." Hesitating, he added, "We're offering you an opportunity to work with one of the best. Can you afford to pass that up?"

"Ordinarily, no, but—"

"Then let me give you another reason to say yes. The man himself." He hesitated again, this time as though he were deciding whether or not to take her into his confidence. "His forebears are in the French history books. You probably knew he was aristocracy. The gossip columns milked that story dry right after he won his first Oscar. After he was blacklisted, most of them didn't bother to report that he'd thrown it all over—title, land, everything. His deceased father was the Marquis de Villefors. . . ."

As Paul went on, Sasha touched the fine gold chain at her neck, running her thumb over the small diamond in the charm.

It was ironic that Paul Maxwell was trying to seduce her with the very man she'd targeted as trouble. He couldn't know that it wasn't Marc's background that intrigued her nearly as much as the chance to work with one of the best. What was more irresistible to an actor than the opportunity to work with a virtuoso director? Could she pass that up? A pulse ticked in her throat.

"Well, Sasha, what do you think?"

Maxwell's quietly voiced question pulled at her. She looked up at Gemini's production chief and smiled. "I think I'd like that drink now."

The next day an elderly houseboy let Sasha into the Malibu beach house. He looked as old as Confucius in his white, surgically clean smock coat, and was probably just as wise, she decided.

"Where should I put these?" the limo driver asked, arriving in the doorway with her bags.

The houseboy motioned him toward a free-standing stairway that seemed suspended on air, then he darted up the steps to the first landing, turned, and smiled.

"Follow him?" Sasha suggested. She supposed she should follow them, too, if she wanted to know where her room was, but the view from where she stood had captured her attention.

Her heart, her senses, quickened in response to the beauty. Drawn slowly toward a thirty-foot-high wall of glass, she looked down over sun-bleached cliffs to the relentless roll of high tide battering against the rocks below. Magnificent, she thought, feeling a tug of something elemental inside her.

Her gaze softened as she stared down, details blurring as white cliffs, blue sea, and sky blended like watercolors framed in a halo of fuzzy white light. A quietness touched her, gentle, enveloping. Her eyes misted, stinging pleasurably. A second or two elapsed before the soft thud of footsteps roused her.

"Anything else you need, miss?" the limo driver called out, clumping down the stairs.

Sasha swiped at her cheek and turned unsteadily, feeling caught and suddenly foolish as he came toward her.

"You okay? Miss?"

She saw herself in the reflection of his dark glasses, saw the bright sad blink of her own eyes. "Sure. Thanks for taking the bags up."

"No problem." Smiling awkwardly, he took off his glasses, revealing tiny close-set eyes. "Name's Bink," he said, "any problems, you call me. I'm out in the guest house. I guess they told you

you're not supposed to leave except to go to the studio. And don't answer the phone. In fact, they'd rather you didn't use the phone at all unless there's an emergency."

He left by the louvered French doors that opened onto a terrace. The colonel would approve of the way they keep this place up, she thought, looking around for the houseboy. When he didn't appear, she began to explore her surroundings.

The living room tempered the celestial grandeur of its floor-to-rafter windows with warm, hardwood floors, faded Persian carpets, and antiques upholstered in rich, satiny brocades. Armloads of fresh-cut flowers were in lead-crystal vases.

Sasha wandered down a short, skylighted hallway, through a gleaming kitchen, and into a bedroom suite that took her breath away. This has to be Leslie's room, she thought, feeling like an interloper. It was an Arabian Nights fantasy in shades of peach and gold, much too opulent for Sasha's taste, but breathtaking nevertheless.

A picture, framed in gilt, stood on a white Bombay desk to Sasha's right. She stepped closer, mesmerized by the couple's unsmiling pose. The man was Marc-André Renaud. The woman—her hair white-blond, her eyes as languid as reflecting pools—could have been Sasha McCleod!

Apprehension curled inside Sasha. She drew back from the picture like a fragile clover drawing into itself at dusk. Shivering, she couldn't take her eyes off the sensual tableau. Marc, his hand tangled in the woman's hair at her nape, was staring down at her. Light played dramatic tricks with his features, flickering a nuance of cruelty along the classic lines of his mouth, offsetting the harshness with the shadowy melancholy in his pale eyes.

The picture's startling black and white tones created an illusion of such mystical sensuality that Sasha could feel it alter her breathing. *Leslie Parrish*, she told herself. But it was impossible not to see, not to imagine herself in that pose. Impossible not to imagine that man looking down at her, touching her . . .

She backed away slowly, her heart a flurry of wing beats in her chest. Only as she reached the door to the hallway did she realize that someone was in the room with her.

Three

Sasha whirled around and saw an indistinct form poised in a shaft of sun from the skylight. Her breath welled up in her throat.

"Who is it?" she asked.

As he stepped out of the sun, tiny, bowed, and blinking, she nearly sagged to the floor. The *houseboy*.

"Dear God," she said, slumping against the doorjamb, her head coming to rest against the lacquered wood. "You'll never know how badly you startled me. How long have you been here?"

His alert eyes told her he'd probably been there for some time. He lifted a shoulder noncommittally, and at the same time crooked his finger, urging her to follow him.

When she could gather herself together, she did. "Lead on," she said with the resigned irony of a woman who has lost control of her life. "Take me to Nirvana, or wherever else happens to be on the itinerary this morning."

They ascended the stairs and traveled a long hallway toward the ocean end of the house. Trudging behind him dutifully, Sasha figured out he must be taking her to her room.

They entered a French country drawing room, its centerpiece a brass daybed dressed up in deep Bordeau red, navy blue, and creams. Two cherrywood wing chairs sat by a large multipaned window, and a regal ficus in a Portuguese planter reached nearly to the ceiling.

Perfectly charming, Sasha thought, peering through opened double doors at a bed canopied in eggshell French voile, and beyond the bedroom, to a small, sunny alcove that housed a writing desk and chair.

The houseboy began opening drawers and closets as she entered the bedroom, showing her that he'd unpacked her things and put them all away. Glancing at panties meticulously stacked in a paper-lined dresser drawer, Sasha sighed. A man after my own heart, she thought. He knows how to fold.

"Thank you," she said, subduing the urge to hug him. Serenely she walked through the alcove and out onto the terrace. The view was every bit as beautiful as before. Steeped in the seacoast's rippling blue majesty, she only gradually became aware that the room had grown silent. She turned around and found the houseboy gone.

It hit Sasha some fifteen minutes later, after she'd thoroughly appreciated her immaculate surroundings, that she had nowhere to go and nothing to do. The picture she'd seen downstairs flashed to mind, piquing her curiosity. The woman with Marc had to be Leslie, but where was she now? And what had caused them to end their relationship? Sasha turned the questions over in her mind. Any more exploring seemed out of the question with the houseboy lurking around.

Ten more minutes ticked by, and her French country suite began to feel like San Quentin done up in chintz. She had a million questions and no one to pose them to. She couldn't even use the phone.

She slipped on a leotard and whiled away a few more minutes with stretching exercises. Then, gazing longingly out the terrace windows, she decided, somewhat desperately, to risk another tour of the premises. Perhaps she'd get some sense of the place and its inhabitants.

She hit pay dirt with the first door she opened. "Good grief," she murmured, startled. The spacious room might have been beautiful once. At the moment the scene looked like the morning after the Roman festival of Bacchus. A semi-circular bar was stocked with fifths of every kind of liquor imaginable, most of them standing half full along the bar top. Overflowing ashtrays dotted tables and straddled chair arms, their stale stench burning into Sasha's nostrils.

A couch was strewn with newspapers, legal pads, and trade magazines. On a marble-topped coffee table, a half-eaten sandwich and an opened bottle of beer languished.

It was a disaster in need of a woman's hand, and Sasha's own hands twitched with unrequited urges. The satisfaction her soul would receive from seeing this place squeak and sparkle with cleanliness was intoxicating.

Sasha steeled herself against the bewitchment and inched back toward the door. Her foot snagged on something, and she looked down to see a glass ashtray tipped beneath the toe of her shoe, its contents leaking out all over her Reeboks. She swallowed, felt sweat break out on her brow, and whispered a hoarse, "Oh, God." Helpless, she dropped to her knees, frantically brushed off her shoes, whisking up butts and burnt matches as she swept away ashes with her fingers.

Was there such a thing as a perfectionist's hotline, she wondered despairingly. Blotting up the last of the gray powder with a damp finger, she knew it was too late. Even the pros couldn't save her now. The beast was loose. She dusted the residue off her hand, looked around the room, and planned her attack.

"Dig in, McCleod. Latrines first," she said, savoring one of her father's militarisms. Collecting loose debris in a wastepaper basket, she worked her way toward the room's messy center of gravity, the couch.

The newspapers could go, she decided, but perhaps she'd better save the trade magazines and certainly the legal pads. Curious, she picked up one and began to flip through it, more certain with every line that it was Marc's handwriting.

Translating the masculine shorthand, she said aloud, "An establishing shot on the beach . . . a wide pan along the coastline at dawn . . . zoom in on dead body washing in the tidal foam. . . ."

A chill shook her at the image—and at the knowledge that she was reading his directorial notes. It felt uncomfortably like snooping in a private journal. Caught in the squeeze between conscience and curiosity, she continued flipping through the pages until she came to what appeared to be a story overview.

She read, her voice dropping to a whisper, "Natural antagonists, Jesse and Lisa are caught in a nightmare. Jesse has been convicted of murder and sentenced to life. Lisa is the rookie cop who helped bring him to justice. He takes her hostage, uses her to escape and to find the man who framed him. He's wounded and suddenly Lisa's in control. Does she turn him in? Does she help him?"

Transfixed, Sasha flipped the page and continued. "The sexual tension is high. In a shattering choice, Lisa betrays her professional ethics and her deepest loyalties and chooses Jesse. Their passion is the desperate wildness of a man and woman who are risking everything—and may not live to love again."

Breathing faster, Sasha read on, poring over the scribbled description of a love scene passionate beyond anything she'd ever imagined. "Jesse tears off Lisa's ragged dress as she drops to her knees in front of him. Tangling his hand in her hair, he lifts her to him and kisses her with all the harrowing hunger in his soul. . . ."

A fist pounded in Sasha's chest, a damp film covered her body as she read on and on, devouring a love scene so emotionally wrenching, so wild and beautiful, it left her trembling with excitement.

Somewhere in the house a door slammed.

To Sasha's taut nerves it was a crack of thunder. She dropped the legal pad and whirled around, every cell of her mind registering the sound of footsteps climbing the stairway, striding down the hall toward her.

This time Sasha knew who it was. And it didn't matter that she could hear him coming or that she was anticipating his appearance in the doorway. When he flashed into view, strangely surreal and compelling, his eyes as desolately beautiful as ice crystals, she started like a frightened animal and stumbled backward.

Lord, she thought, does this man know how to make an entrance! "Do you always have to storm a room?" she asked, taking the offensive.

As Marc Renaud's wintry gaze swept over her,

she took another step back. "Well, what's wrong?" she asked, her calves pressed up against the couch behind her.

Ignoring the question, he hestitated in the doorway and considered Sasha's leotard-swathed body. Dispassionately taking in her hardening nipples, he asked quietly, "Cold?"

Sasha's eyes flicked down and up again just as quickly. Heat pooled in her face; color tinted her throat. "Ever worn a damp leotard, Mr. Renaud? Yes, I'm cold."

His expression softened as he surveyed the room. Slipping his hands into his pants pockets, he considered the sparkling bar at length, his lower lip drawing in thoughtfully at one corner.

Sasha relaxed her defenses a bit. Perhaps he wasn't angry. Perhaps he'd just *looked* angry. Feeling generous, she granted that a man couldn't be held responsible for the fact that he'd been born with the eyes of a mythic god of wrath and hellfire.

He settled his gaze on her again, a Gallic shimmer of confusion in his features. "Why?"

Unexpected, his half-whispered word swept through Sasha's barriers like winds through a field of wheat. The way he said it, it could have meant anything. *Why are you so beautiful? Why am I inescapably drawn to you? Why do I want you so badly? Why?* As he gestured around the room, she forced herself to acknowledge that he meant her cleaning spree. "I had to," she said, lifting her shoulders. "It was so dirty."

Marc was looking at her with skeptical fascination. "Arturo called me. He told me you were . . . cleaning. A madwoman, he said."

Sasha might have taken issue if her conscience hadn't snuck up and ambushed her. Her guilt was tenfold. Not only had she given in to her demons, but Marc clearly didn't appreciate her frenzied efforts. Brought down by a dirty ashtray, she thought, sighing. "Who's Arturo?"

"My houseboy."

"I guess you're one of those types who needs disorder to create?"

"Something like that," he said, dropping his suit jacket over the nearest chair and walking toward the bar.

Sasha couldn't help but notice the dramatic change in his appearance. In charcoal gray suit pants, and a white shirt open at the neck, he looked as though he'd come from an obligatory lunch with the film's foreign investors. His tie was pulled loose, its tails hanging down his shirtfront. It was a comfortable image on most American males, but oddly, on him, a European, it gave off Wall Street–like waves of power.

Watching him pour brandy into a sparkling snifter, one of several that she'd saved from the blight of water spots, Sasha ran a finger along the neckline of her leotard and lifted the material away from her moist skin.

He swirled the brandy once, watched its colors flash in the light. "Don't ever interfere with this room again," he said, startling her with the quiet force of his voice.

He looked up slowly, pinning her with his gaze, seeming to speak directly to her pounding heart. "Disorder I can take or leave. What I can't take, Sasha, what I *don't* need, is mothering."

Even as he said the last word she caught a glimpse of something in his features, a nuance so quick she couldn't describe it, yet it stunned her. It could have been that same melancholy she'd seen in the picture, the fleeting sadness that only a high-speed camera could have captured. She knew only that her senses had registered something—and that her stomach was twisting.

All the air in the room seemed to have disappeared. She was caught in a vacuum that snared the silence, stretching it taut. A question filled Sasha's mind, and she gave in to an impulse. "Am I very much like her? Like Leslie?" she asked.

Now it was Marc Renaud's turn to be confused. He stared at Sasha's rich, strange eyes, the golden halo of hair wisping around her face where it had strayed loose from the restraints of its thick braid, and thought that no one could be less like Leslie than she. Given the events of current weeks, he'd lost all respect for his missing star, personally and professionally—he'd lost all tender feelings for her long ago. He harbored no such disrespect for Sasha. Quite the opposite.

Whether it came out of his directorial skills or some other less-practiced instinct, Marc Renaud often knew things about people they didn't know themselves. What he knew about the tawny, long-limbed blonde across the room disturbed and compelled him. She was an endangered species, he suspected, an uncompromising woman caught in a world that existed by compromise. If he was right about her, she would fight at the drop of a hat for something she believed in, reasonable or not, fashionable or not. Under other circumstances Marc might have admired that quality in her—or in anyone. It was rare enough in his business.

But he had a picture to salvage.

Make that a career, he thought grimly.

He swirled the brandy again, drank from its perfumed heat. Fortunately he sensed something else in her. There was a quiver of uncertainty hidden beneath her fire and pride. Sasha McCleod was a fraction less sure of the world than she appeared.

That tiny flaw was all he needed.

"You're nothing like Leslie," he said, keeping his voice neutral, "except for the physical resemblance. That may be enough for our purposes, then again . . ." Letting the sentence hang, he walked to the chair where he'd dropped his coat, took out a pack of Gauloises, and glanced at her. "Mind?"

"Yes," she said, the quiver of uncertainty now evident in her voice. "I do mind."

After a second's hesitation he tapped out a cigarette and lit it with a lighter from his jacket. Glancing at her, he took a long drag and let the smoke curl up into his nostrils. What would the woman who'd been known to pluck cigarettes out of men's mouths do now, he wondered.

She stiffened, struggling with her convictions. Her eyes shot darts of fire.

He took another drag and walked toward her, aware of the flush that stained her cheeks. Bending to crush the cigarette out in an ashtray on the coffee table, he said, "Let's talk about the movie."

"By all means," she said, her body taut as a bowstring.

He sprawled at one end of the couch, and she sat on its opposite arm, resistance knit into her posture.

Marc drew his tie off and dropped it on the table. Uncompromising? he thought, almost chuckling. She looked like a ramrod drill sergeant perched there on the couch. At ease, he wanted to tell her.

Her obstinance triggered an awareness. He was used to seeing respect, even a little fear, in an actress's eyes. What would it take, he wondered, to bring that kind of vulnerability to her eyes? The question ignited a strange sensation inside him. His first impulse was to touch her gently, to bring warmth to her porcelain skin. Lord, the urge was almost painful. It squeezed off his breath for a second.

Without warning, a second impulse came in its wake, much more primitive and powerful, an ancient male need for mastery in matters of rebellion and women. He subdued the reaction before it could ignite the spark in his loins. Hungry for a cigarette, he turned away and fed his addictive nerves with a deep breath of oxygen instead. Lord, she had an uncanny effect on him. He'd never experienced anything like it before.

"Do you know anything about how I work?" he asked finally.

"Extensive rehearsal," she replied without hesitation. "I've read that's your style. And lots of takes, as many as it requires to get the shot you want."

"You've been reading the entertainment columns. At least they're half right this time. I do use rehearsal, but I want the shot on the first take if I can get it. That's when everything's sharp-edged and new." Sensing the relaxation of her posture, he sat forward on the couch. "Of course, in your case, none of the rules apply. We'll be using every trick in the book to get what we need. I've even arranged for some coaching."

Her eyes reflected interest.

"For the next two days," he told her, "you'll be working with voice and acting coaches. You'll be watching videotapes of Leslie's work and, of course, you'll see all the footage we've shot so far. . . ."

Sasha listened, her rigidity dissipating. Suddenly their plan for her to take Leslie Parrish's place in a picture was more than just a crazy fantasy. It was a crazy reality.

"I'd like more time to prepare you," he said, "but the picture's already over budget and behind schedule."

She smiled. "That's okay. I didn't expect two days." Paul had been right about him, she realized. There was an odd passion in his voice when he talked about his picture. It humanized him, even melted the coldness in his eyes a little. Suddenly she became acutely aware of the way he propped his foot up on the rung of the coffee table and was leaning into it, the contours of hard thigh muscle beneath the fabric of his slacks, and particularly the dusting of dark curly hair that was flirting with the open neckline of his shirt. He would have to have fabulous body hair, wouldn't he? she thought.

"I've got a videotape of Leslie that I think you ought to see. It was taken a year ago in Tahiti, on location for our last film. It's the woman I want you to study, not the actress."

Sasha nodded, curious, and at the same time strangely unsettled at the possibility of seeing Marc and Leslie together in paradise. What had gone wrong between them? Sasha studied his profile as he leafed through the legal pad she'd been snooping in earlier. He didn't have the look of a star-crossed lover as he stopped at the movie overview she'd read and skimmed it silently. He had the look of a man completely preoccupied with his pet project.

"We'll have to reshoot the love scene first," he said more to himself than to her. "And we'll pick up the rest of the studio shots as quickly as possible. Gemini is tightening the screws. They're leasing the Paramount lot at an astronomical rate."

"Love scene?"

"Shouldn't present a problem," he assured her, glancing up. "We'll film it from various angles, avoiding close-ups of your face."

Tension curled inside her. If he meant the love scene she'd read earlier, the paper it was written on would sizzle if a drop of water hit it! It was emotional and beautiful, yes, but she wasn't at all sure she could play it with the wild abandon it called for. "Paul told me I was being hired for action shots, swimming, long-distance running, that sort of thing."

"Paul isn't this picture's director," he said, an edge of impatience in his voice. "He doesn't understand the editing process. I've been reviewing footage, and I've decided there are scenes that have to be reshot. It's that simple."

"But the love scene. Isn't that crucial?"

"It's the pivotal point of the movie. Unfortunately Leslie played it as if it were a visit to her dentist."

Tension curled again, a slipknot pulling tighter as Sasha struggled against it. "I see . . . and would that be the nude scene you were referring to at the audition?"

"Normally, yes, but for you we'll work something out. A flesh-colored leotard, maybe," he said, smiling, his eyes straying momentarily to her breasts. "You seem to like leotards."

He hadn't touched her, but he might as well have for the way Sasha reacted. A flush tingled her skin, and she felt warm, short of breath. "I'm an actress," she insisted, her voice faint, her pride involved. "I don't need a flesh-colored leotard."

Marc blinked and grew still, disbelief mingling with irritation. He rose, walked to the bar, lit a cigarette, and took a quick drag. "I'm a director," he said, a stream of smoke issuing out with the words, "and under the circumstances I've decided to forego the nudity in that scene."

"What circumstances?"

Go easy, he cautioned himself silently, settling his cigarette in the nearest ashtray. He'd dealt with prima donnas before. Most of them needed reassurance, some needed a swift kick in the derriere. This one, he decided, needed to be reasoned with. But another image seared his thoughts before he could stop it. A rearing palomino, her graceful legs pawing the air, her cornsilk mane flying as she refused the bit. A white-gold animal with a spirit too strong to be broken.

He swallowed what felt like a soft groan in his throat.

She stood up. "What circumstances?" she repeated.

"Think about it, Sasha," he said, his voice rougher than he'd intended. "There'll be enough tension on the set without imposing a nude scene on an untested actress." Approaching her, he added quietly, "It's not you, believe me. I'd have to do this no matter who we brought in. A tense set equals a lousy picture."

He watched the fire dart in her eyes, and again the image of a shying golden horse overwhelmed him. Again his urge was to gentle her, to quiet her frantic heart under his hands, to melt her limbs to the wild honey he used to love. . . .

It's not you, palomino, it's me.

Thinking he saw relief in her eyes, he felt an answering response in his muscles. The truth was he couldn't handle having her naked anywhere near his set. Looking at her, he knew two things. He'd been right when she'd asked Paul Maxwell to get him another actress for the picture. She had the power to distract him, to foul his creative instincts. She promised to be the final disaster in a series of disasters.

Another truth rocked through him as he walked to the bar to pour himself another drink. It crackled loudly in his brain. It roared like a brushfire, flaring through him, galvanizing his nerves. *He wanted her.* The impulse was ancient, primitive, and powerful. It was new and painful and sweet. He wanted her like he'd never wanted a woman before in his life.

Four

"The conflict is eating you up inside, okay?" said the blond, boyish acting instructor who'd been working with Sasha for the last two days. Crouched by the arm of Sasha's makeup chair, he added, "You're desperately in love with the fugitive that *you* helped bring to justice, and it's tearing you apart."

"Desperately in love—" Sasha mouthed the words, provoking her makeup man into a sigh of annoyance. The ponytailed cosmetician cranked her head around and applied another smudge of purple shadow under her eyes. She had to look gaunt and beautiful and deeply troubled for the upcoming scene, which shouldn't be too difficult, she allowed, given her lack of sleep and jittery state of mind.

Sasha hated nerves in any form. She had no patience with anxiety attacks whatsoever, and so when they came, always unbidden and at the worst possible moments in her life, she had precious few coping mechanisms at her disposal. Nerves were her Achilles heel, her undoing. Given a choice at birth, she would gladly have foregone a nervous system altogether if an alternative had been available. As it was, she accepted nature's burden, made the best of it—and wore her locket.

Only half listening to her coach, she reached for the antique gold heart, but her fingers found only the warm, bare skin of her throat. Anxiety crested again as she remembered she'd been told not to wear any jewelry for the scene. This was to be their first day of actual filming, and though no one had said as much to her, she knew the movie sank or swam by her performance. Could she do a convincing Lisa? Could she do a convincing Leslie *doing* Lisa?

"You're risking *everything*," her young instructor was explaining fervently, "your profession, your personal ethics, even your life. You're going against your own instincts, Lisa"—he paused to let her register the name of her character—"and you're doing it for love."

"Love." Sasha risked the makeup man's ire to glance down at her coach. "I think I understand Lisa's conflict. I'm just not sure I can convey it."

He stood and squeezed her hand as though to transfuse her with his boundless confidence. "You can. Just be there, Sasha, be in the moment. Let your feelings exist, acknowledge them, express them, and you'll be terrific."

Sasha caught her own reflection in the mirror as the makeup man angled her head up and began etching a nasty-looking scratch on her cheek. Let her feelings exist? She was flirting with a full-blown panic attack!

"Be there, Sasha!" Her coach headed for the door, flashed her a thumbs-up sign, and disappeared.

Abandoned, Sasha mentally replayed the scene

they were going to shoot. She'd arrived early to run lines with Carlos, her leading man, who had impressed her as a brooding type with artistic temperament to spare. He was always muttering about his instrument and finding his center. If he was upset about redoing the love scene with Sasha, he didn't bother to mention it. In fact, she had the distinct feeling he thought she *was* Leslie. Self-absorbed, she decided, remembering not to smile, that was the word for Carlos. Furiously self-absorbed.

Moments later, making her way through the cavernous sound stage to the set, Sasha drew in a steadying breath. Much as she wanted to deny it, the prospect of working with Marc Renaud accounted for at least ninety percent of her nerves. She hadn't seen him since their conversation in the beach house, and despite his brief attack of sensitivity then, she had no reason to think he'd be anything but icy and autocratic on the set. No doubt she made things worse between them with her bred-in-the-bone aversion to authority. They seemed to be natural adversaries, destined to clash unless one of them could learn to defer gracefully. *Don't bet the rent it'll be him,* she thought, tugging the fraying collar of her costume into place.

A hunk of cotton broadcloth came off in her hand. She stopped dead, stared at it, and moaned softly. The other ten percent of her nerves could be blamed directly on the tattered rag of a dress that Carlos soon would be ripping off her in a fit of passion. The flimsy breakaway shirtwaist already exposed an entire shoulder, half a breast, and three quarters of her left thigh. One careless move, and it probably would drop to her ankles of its own accord.

That awful possibility vanished as the first object of Sasha's concerns came into view. The set was buzzing with activity, and Marc Renaud was at the center of it. She stopped to watch and to give herself a moment to adjust to being on a bona fide movie set complete with an internationally acclaimed director. This is it, she thought, compressing her lips. Her shoulders rose and fell with a sharp, anticipatory breath. *Break a leg.*

Renaud was talking to his script supervisor and his camera operator simultaneously as Sasha moved to the fringes of the commotion. He hadn't seen her yet, so she took the opportunity to check out his mood before she approached him.

His voice was too low for her to catch the words, but she could read the single-mindedness in his expression, the take-charge intensity in his gestures. This was a man who ruled his turf. *His* turf, she thought uneasily, glancing around the low-lit set—and he probably issued orders with all the warmth and sensitivity of a feudal warlord.

Ironically, by his clothes she might have taken him for one of the near-impoverished people in downtown L.A. The worn denims and baggy sweater spoke of his indifference to style, but they didn't offset his innate aristocratic bearing or the classic bones of his profile. His high forehead and narrowly bridged nose had the dimensions of an ancient Greek statue.

It was his wideset mouth that seemed to break the rules of noble birth. The shaded curve of his upper lip settled almost angrily on a full, sensual lower lip. Fascinated, she found herself wondering if his mouth expressed the two opposing sides of his nature.

Her heart began to beat harder as she moved in closer then hesitated when the script supervisor glanced her way and whispered something to Marc.

She'd been spotted, she realized, stiffening as Marc turned to look at her. She locked up when she was nervous, and worse, she became too assertive. "Good morning," she managed softly, determined not to fall into a defensive mode with him.

Marc considered her for a moment, his eyes narrowing. Finally he nodded an acknowledgment and went back to his conversation.

Sasha teetered on the brink of disbelief. He wasn't going to say a word, not *one* word? She'd had no idea how much his acceptance meant to her until that moment. The jolt of disappointment sharpened into hurt, anger, and the quick sting of wounded pride. Before she could get the chain reaction in hand, it had set off her damn nerves again! She walked to the portable coffee bar and mixed herself a cup of sugar-free cocoa. Well, what did she expect from a man who thought she was too tall and couldn't take direction, she asked herself—the star treatment? Sipping the hot, tasteless brew, she ordered herself to concentrate on her lines—and on regaining her emotional equilibrium.

What Sasha didn't know, couldn't have known, was the dramatic effect she'd had on Marc Renaud's equilibrium. Signaling for one of his assistant directors to field the crews' questions, Marc stepped back, away from the free-for-all for a moment, to quiet his ricocheting thoughts—and to get another look at her.

In costume and makeup Sasha's physical resemblance to Leslie was uncanny. It had caught him like an unexpected blow to the chest when he'd first seen her. Not that he could ever mistake her for Leslie. No, not by any stretch. Leslie's appeal was her kittenish sensuality. Sasha's was her fiery, hands-off *sexuality*. Beyond that, she had a strength and spirit about her that was almost tensile, a purity of purpose that could take a man's breath away. They emanated from her, those qualities. They shone around her like a halo.

The dress that hung on her revealed every graceful line of her tawny, long-limbed body, and it also revealed her state of tension. The muscles of her stomach were drawn tight as steel bands, and the nipples of her breasts were budded against the thin fabric. It wasn't cold in the room, not under the lights, he remarked to himself with a mirthless smile. No, she was nervous, *very* nervous.

That suited his purposes for the day's scene. He needed her vulnerable, even frightened, if that could be arranged. Her character, Lisa, had to be on the ragged edges, riddled with fears and doubts, half crazy with pent-up love and passion. She couldn't be played by a woman with a dead-bolt on her life and her destiny. He'd known all along the kinds of casting problems Sasha would present. He'd even tried to explain them to Paul Maxwell. She was too "together" to play Lisa. In order for this scene to work, she would have to unravel emotionally, come apart at the seams. That would require some inspired acting, he thought, glancing at his watch.

"Okay, company," he called out, raising his hand, "let's see what kind of damage we can do today. Sasha—"

She turned to him, startled, a sparkle of apprehension in her eyes. "What?" she asked, her hand drawing up protectively, covering the breast that was partially exposed. It was as though he'd threatened her somehow simply by saying her name. For a second he thought she might be about to gasp, a tiny, sexy puff of sound, and his body responded as though she had. The cords of his neck tightened and a chill ran down his arms.

"Let's get to work," he said flatly, "I'd like you and Carlos to walk through the scene a couple of times."

Marc waved her onto the set and pointed a finger at Carlos. "You're on the bed, semi-conscious, Carlos, and Sasha is standing over you. Sasha, remember, you hold this man's fate in your hands."

Sasha positioned herself by the bed, her hand still hovering protectively in the area of her breast. Smiling to himself, Marc wondered what she was going to do when Carlos ripped that dress off her during the actual filming. It should be quite a moment, he thought, especially since she obviously did not have on the body stocking she'd been told to wear.

What was underneath the dress, he wondered, more aware than he wanted to be of her willowy lines and curves. His stomach tightened as a subliminal flash hit him, an unbidden vision of her lithe, beautiful body . . . *nude*.

His breathing altered for a moment, became deep and protracted.

In the time it took him to shake off the image, the set activity had slowed to a crawl as the crew waited for him. Ignoring the knot in his stomach, Marc walked to the bed to give Carlos a couple of pointers on his motivation. Finally, every inch the cold, pragmatic director again, he turned to Sasha.

"This man's life is hanging in the balance," he told her, perhaps with a little more force than necessary. He could see the tension in her features, and he needed to get through to her, to communicate the pivotal urgency of the scene. "Can you feel that, Sasha? Can you feel the power of Lisa's position? Her horror of making the wrong choice?"

"I think so—"

"Say it like you mean it."

She blinked, a snap of light in her eyes. "I've read the script, Mr. Renaud, several times. I understand the story and the character."

"Marc," he suggested quietly, "it seems to work better all around when people call me Marc." He stepped back, held out a hand. "If you're ready, then."

Marc knew he'd shaken her up. He'd intended to. There was a good chance he'd have to shake her up again. He needed honest gut emotion for this scene, and if that meant baiting her, then that's what he'd do. Actors were intriguing, unpredictable creatures, and he'd learned to use whatever worked. He nurtured when that got him what he wanted, he intimidated, he enticed. He worked best with actors who had the inner security to surrender themselves to the scene—and to the director.

Watching Sasha now, tracking her as she walked to Carlos's supine body, he knew she would resist any obvious "handling." The insecurities were there, but she covered them with an independence that bordered on rebellion. Why, he wondered. Had she been taught to do so by the military father Paul had mentioned? Whatever the reason, there was something rigid in her, some need to prove she was in control.

For one unchecked second his mind darted back into dangerous territory. What would it be like with her, he wondered. With this fiercely independent female? Would she be as frantic and sweet as he imagined? Would she cry out when he entered her? Or would she arch and sigh and entwine him in those long, long legs?

The last image cut into him like a knife. The sharp sensation in his gut left him short of breath and taut as a cocked gun. He stood there a moment, feeling it, fighting it, bringing himself under control, willing himself sane.

Moments later he *was* sane. Sheer force of will, the survival mechanism he'd honed and perfected in the blackest moments of his past, had cut out the impulse with a scalpel's precision. Only a faint tripping of his pulse remained.

Moving into the shadows, he observed silently, letting Sasha run through the entire scene with Carlos. He wanted to see what she could do without interference. He had her pegged as too inflexible for any real acting range, but for the sake of the picture, he half hoped she would pull a rabbit out of the hat and prove him wrong. *Surprise me*, he thought as she hesitated at the door of the cabin, caught in the conflict of Lisa's agonizing decision.

Halfway into it, Marc knew she was giving it her best despite the nerves, that she could never give anything less, and the grudging respect of one strong competitor for another built inside him. She was proud. She was beautiful. She was spectacular, but, dammit, she was one lousy actress. Her facial expression was wooden, her movements stiff and hopelessly self-conscious.

"Hold it!" he called out. "Sasha, come here." He waved her over. "Take five," he told the cast and crew.

He took her by the arm and drew her aside, aware of the resistance in her body—and the quickening energy in his own. "The first thing I want you to do is relax," he told her, careful to keep his voice low, his own responses in check. "You're making it happen. Do you know what I mean by that, Sasha? I want you to *let* it happen. Don't perform, give yourself over to the role. Don't do Lisa, *be* Lisa."

"I'm trying," she insisted softly.

"I know." Her warm, firm flesh gave under the slight pressure of his fingers. "Too hard, Sasha. You're trying too hard. Let it happen."

She quieted, met his gaze, and her expression softened. He could feel her opening up, surrendering a little. He smiled at her faintly, and something happened through their eyes, some transference of mental energy, some fusion of understanding. For an instant Marc's breath got trapped somewhere in his chest. He felt connected, linked to her by a grounding current of electricity. This was more than a director advising his star, it was male and female, an instinctive communication between the sexes. The cords of his neck contracted, and the effect rippled down his muscles like a wave. What arrested him most was the wonderment in her expression, the whiskey hues in her eyes. She was wildly, incredibly beautiful.

"Let it happen?" She glanced down at his hand, a hushed, sensual tremor in her voice.

An impulse flashed through Marc, primal, straight out of the evolutionary past—the biological urge to take, to conquer and possess. *He wanted her now, on the floor, beneath him. He wanted to bury himself inside her, this golden woman he'd done nothing more to than touch—*

He stifled the urge as quickly as it hit him, but she must have seen it in his eyes, felt it in his grip on her arm. She drew back, blinking at him with that startled look he'd seen before. It occurred to him that he hadn't released her yet, that he had to let go of her. When he did, the current of electricity arced up his arm.

He heard the normal buzz of activity behind him on the set, but he was totally disconnected from it. Lord, what had just happened, he wondered. This time his willpower hadn't cut off the response. This time it was taking him more than a moment to recover. His heart pounding hard, he stared at her until finally the director in him overrode the man. "All right—" he called out to the milling crew, "let's try it again."

Riptides of tension permeated the set from that point on. Even the crew talked in hushed tones, as though a loud voice might set some unknowable and irreversible chain reaction of events in motion. Marc called for rehearsal after rehearsal, forcing Sasha and Carlos to play the scene repeatedly, sometimes from the beginning, occasionally from a problem area, but always with the unspoken demand that they give more of themselves.

Sasha's responses remained unnatural and self-conscious, but Marc was relentless. He believed now that she had it in her to do the scene right. The capability was there. It was locked up as tight as a teenager's diary, but it was *there*, the emotion, the conflicted passion—everything she needed.

They worked straight through lunch, and by midafternoon, with the production crew ready to mutiny, Marc called a break. Sasha collapsed on the bed of the set as the cast and crew departed. Trembling from the strain of the morning, limp with emotional fatigue, she closed her eyes. She was too drained and upset to think about eating.

Hearing someone approach, she took a deep breath and opened her eyes. She knew it was Marc, and she'd been waiting for this moment. Pent-up frustration escaped her like steam from a simmering tea kettle. "We're running this scene into the ground," she said, staring at his shadowy form by the foot of the bed. "Why? It was better twenty times ago. I'm exhausted."

"That's why." He came into the light, pointed to the reddening stains on her face. "I wanted this from you, what you're feeling now—*emotion*, the real thing. The question you should ask yourself is why I had to exhaust you to get to it."

He leaned against the brass bed frame and folded his arms, revealing some of his own weariness. "A little advice? When you get to the end of your rope, Sasha, don't tie a knot and hang on. *Let go.* Do you understand? Let go, take the fall." His voice softened. "I'm trying to get you prepared for the camera. When the camera is ready, *you* have to be ready."

"I'll be ready for a convalescent home! I can't believe you put all your actors through this."

"Not all of them. Just you."

"Just me?" She looked him up and down. "What's that supposed to mean?"

"It means—" He broke off, shook his head as though he weren't sure the explanation was worth the effort.

"You're not going to tell me?" she asked, furious.

He swung around. "It means," he said, grabbing her wrist and pulling her toward him, "that you are willful, self-centered, and rebellious to the point of idiocy. It means that I've lost another half day's shooting because of you. And it also means that you're devoid of talent, McCleod. That's right," he reiterated as she gazed up at him in shock, "as actresses go, you stink."

He released her abruptly and turned to leave, adding over his shoulder, "We start rehearsing again in forty-five minutes. Be here."

Sasha watched him stride toward the side exit, her heart thundering in her chest. If he'd meant to infuriate her, he'd sure as hell succeeded. As he reached the door, she sprang off the bed. "You don't have to waste any more rehearsal time on me, Renaud. I'll get the scene right, dammit!"

He turned and glared at her. "We'll see, McCleod. Personally I don't believe you've got it in you."

Sasha felt tears of sheer exhaustion burning her eyes. "I can do it!" she vowed, her chin trembling violently. "I'll prove it to you. Here"—she grabbed the script up off the bed, flung it back down—"I'll do it now!"

Skepticism hung over him like a storm cloud. "You'll do it now?" he questioned, walking toward her. "Are you telling me that you're ready to strip off the layers of pride, the self-consciousness, that you're not terrified of what's underneath?"

"What are you? A radio psychologist?" she asked, her voice hoarse with fatigue. "I said I can do the scene."

He considered the idea, his eyes assessing her shaking hands, her drawn features. "Fine, I'll read the part of Jesse."

Moments later, immersing herself in the emotional scene, Sasha walked through the door of the set and stared at the bed, vividly imagining Jesse's semi-conscious body sprawled there. Trembling, she approached him, and suddenly it was all terrifyingly real. He was in front of her, bleeding, dying, the hunted, haunted man she'd nearly betrayed. She could hear his ragged breathing, see the fevered flush of his dusky skin. Jesse was dying. He needed her. She was torn with guilt and desperation at the utter hopelessness of it all, rocked with love and longing for him.

"Jesse?" A naked quiver of pain shook her voice.

She stood at the bed and dropped to her knees, reaching out for him, laying her head on the blanket and sobbing. "Jesse," she pleaded, "don't die."

She could almost hear him rouse, feel his body heat as he rolled to his side and grasped her arm. Shuddering violently, she registered the insistent strength of his fingers and gradually realized that it was Marc Renaud who held her, that he was crouched next to her, repeating Jesse's words. "Look at me," he whispered, a brutal tone to his voice, "*look at me, Lisa.*"

A shock wave of physical longing paralyzed her. She couldn't. It didn't matter that the script called for her to look up at Jesse, to mouth his name. Her heart was thudding in her chest, a heavy, hurtful beat. She couldn't look at the man who was rising above her, drawing her up with him.

"Lisa—"

She ripped away from him, pushed to her feet, and stumbled to the far wall of the set.

"What is it? Lisa—what's wrong?"

"I'm sorry," she said, her back to him. She wasn't sure if those were the right words, if she was still acting, if any of it was in the script.

"Sorry? Why? What did you do?" He hesitated, swore under his breath and slowly exhaled Jesse's disbelief. "Not the police? You didn't—"

Whirling around, tears streaming, she was Lisa again. "Yes— "

In her mind he was there, across the room from her . . . Jesse, trying to stand, staggering and sinking back to the bed. Jesse as he clutched the flesh wound at his temple, and blood coated his fingers with crimson. Pain ripped through Sasha's heart. "I didn't tell them where you were, Jesse. I didn't, I *swear*. I hung up."

She walked to him slowly, crying, wanting to

run from him, to escape this man who was tearing her life apart, who was destroying her body and soul. What if he *had* committed the crime he was accused of? What if he'd killed a woman and her child in cold blood?

She hesitated, gasping as he snagged her by the wrist and pulled her to him. With a choked sob she dropped to her knees in front of him, staring up at him . . . mesmerized by the turbulence in his features. Her heart twisted inside her. He looked so lonely, so desperate. And then suddenly it wasn't Jesse's turmoil she was witnessing, it was Marc Renaud's. He was holding her wrist tightly, almost fiercely, and his hand was shaking. In his crystalline blue eyes she saw pain compressed to the hard brilliance of a diamond, a tiny white spot of sadness and rage that she didn't understand and couldn't reach. . . .

What has he done? The question flared into her mind, seared her consciousness like a comet.

"Marc?" she asked, searching his face. She needed to hear his voice, to touch him. She needed to reassure herself that he hadn't metamorphosed into someone else, someone she didn't know at all. "Marc, what is it? Tell me what's wrong. I don't know what to do. . . ."

He exhaled, eased his grip on her wrist, and stared down at her. The emotion was his, but the words he spoke were Jesse's. "Lisa, I need you. Help me—"

His voice caught at the end, broke off as though something vital inside him had snapped.

Tears filled Sasha's eyes again, and the pain inside her mounted. She didn't understand it, the welling sadness, the nearly unbearable longing, but it stung at her lids, ached in her chest. It had nothing to do with the character or the movie—and everything to do with the man and his piercingly beautiful eyes. They ripped through her heart with their breathtaking anguish.

"What is it?" she asked, her fingers at his temple, hovering at the place where the wound would have been. "How can I help you? Tell me what to do." She was desperate to make his pain go away, wild to heal his torment, whatever it was. In her mind he was Marc, but he was Jesse too. She couldn't separate the men or their pain. She was responding to anguish the only way she knew how.

He answered her with a shuddering groan. "I need you," he said again drawing her into the V of his legs. "I'll die without you. . . ." The contact with his body was painful to Sasha's senses. The heat of his enclosing thighs arrested her breathing.

She drew back, staring up at him, silenced by the quivering stricture of her throat. *No, you won't die,* her eyes told him, *I won't let you die. I can be what you need, whatever that is. Please, let me be what you need.*

She reached up to touch his face, and he flinched under her fingers. Tears welled in her eyes. "Jesse, let me be with you," she said, her voice breaking. "Let me make love to you."

His jaw clenched with pain, and a transfiguring wave moved through his features. For an instant, anguish became something else . . . cleansing fire, naked need. Eyes that had burned with death now ignited with life. Awed by the change in him, Sasha trembled with a new emotion, wonderment. A luminescence built inside her, piercing softly, opening her clear to her soul. It was an inner dawn breaking through the darkness and bringing with it the exquisite anticipation of beauty, of hope.

"Angel of death, angel of redemption." Goethe's phrase shook in his throat.

He touched her hand as she caressed his face, and she was seized with longing. She was frantic to be with him, to absorb his pain, to make it her own. It was a bone-deep hunger, a call from the marrow of her being. His hand contracted on her arm, and the heat of it brought a moan of surprise to her lips. Yes, she was frightened, but she understood the fever in him, the desperation. For this moment in time, this split second in the loop of infinity, she was his salvation, his redemption. She could give him back his life.

He caught hold of the bodice of her shirtdress, his voice a serrated plea. "I need you, to touch you." Balling the ragged material in his fist, he slowly dragged her closer to him, a staggering mix of emotion in his eyes. For an instant she saw tenderness there, heartbreaking tenderness. And then in its place, naked desire, waves of it . . . His hands burned her skin, seared her soul. They were hot and hard and rapturously frantic as they worked open the buttons at her neckline. If she hadn't felt the shuddering roughness in his fingers, she would have believed she was dreaming, dying.

Glancing down, she drew in a sharp breath as his fingers slipped through the front placket of her dress and grazed her skin. Her breasts shuddered and tightened instantly, shimmering in anticipation of his touch. Mesmerized, she watched the buttons begin to fall free. The first button, the second. A part of her didn't believe, *couldn't* believe any of it was happening. She was an enthralled child on a roller coaster, and it was too late to stop the plunging momentum.

The third button eluded him. He breathed out a

savage word, and with one magnificent wrench he ripped free a triangle of material, jerking Sasha's body forward with a force that made her cry out. He caught her with one arm and held her suspended, inches from his mouth.

An inner cry of excitement swept her, rioting through her senses. "Dear Lord," she said as her nerves registered his fist tangled in the material at her bodice, his fingers pressed into her trembling flesh. He was a heartbeat away, staring down at her.

The anticipation of his mouth on hers was a fiery ache in her limbs, a cry from deep in her loins. She longed for him to hold her, crush her in his arms, kiss her until she was dizzy and drunk with him. She wanted desperately to know his heat, his fire, his sweetness. She told him so with her eyes, and his response was a shuddering groan, low and beautiful, made brutal with his need.

Disorientation crept into Sasha's senses. It was almost as though he were fighting himself, and that possibility was both thrilling and unnerving to her. That he might have the strength to hold back made her even wilder to be with him. This wasn't about the movie scene anymore, she realized. It was a clash of wills and hearts, a stunning collision of opposite forces, male and female. She felt it all, drank it in until it swamped her, the fear of losing control, the driving desire to be part of him. It was primal and terrifying. *It was real.*

His fingers curled into her hair, his eyes searched out her secrets, but it was his mouth that beguiled her. She saw the whole man there, a microcosm of Marc Renaud in the taut full lines that fought their own sensitivity.

She let her eyes drift from his lips to the pulse

point in his throat. She bent to kiss the tender spot and felt his arms go rigid. He ripped her away from him, held her at arm's length, his hands shaking. "Lord," he whispered, "what are you doing to me?"

The heat of him fled her body, and a convulsive tremor took its place. "I don't know," she said, a sob in her voice. "Dying for you?"

He swept her off the floor as he kissed her, lifting her body to his, crushing her with his intensity. Sasha's world went shock-white for a moment, and then it imploded slowly in a kaleidoscopic burst of color. His mouth, his heartbreakingly soft lips, were the source of light, of beauty.

She wanted to stay forever, spinning in that world of light and beauty . . . she wanted to spiral there like a leaf caught in the wind.

Without warning he released her for an instant, and she was lost in a free fall, plummeting until he caught her to him again. The power in his arms, in his body, intensified her feelings of thrilling, curling weakness. He claimed her lips in a deep, consuming kiss, savage and tender at the same time. His tongue barely touched hers, but she felt its caress deep inside her.

Limp in his arms, she lost touch with her thoughts, her senses, her very heartbeat. The languidness showering her from head to toe was the most beautiful and terrible sensation she had ever had. It felt as though she were dissolving, melting into a pool of fiery liquid. She couldn't call out his name, beg him to stop. She didn't have the strength!

She felt him release the torn material of her dress and slide his fingers inside the ragged opening. She arched up, her hand flying to his arm to stop him, a sigh quivering deep in her throat as he cupped her breast. Her body came alive, electrified. She cried out silently, dizzy with agonized pleasure at the sensations of his fingers on her flesh.

"You make me ache, you're so soft," he whispered against her forehead. And then, relinquishing her breast, he combed his hands into the silky hair at her temples and kissed her with such amazing gentleness, she began to cry. Tears swelled into her eyes.

A line from the script swept into Sasha's thoughts as he shifted back to look at her, words she'd never been able to say convincingly to Carlos. "Jesse"—she breathed out his name on a soft sob—"I love you."

She could feel the recoil in his muscles, could almost see his head snap up as though he'd been hit.

Somewhere in the building a door slammed, and the echo broke through Sasha's languor like a sound traveling through a tunnel, hollowed out and distant. She tightened her fingers on Marc's arm, momentarily confused by the interruption, by his reaction. Her heart caught between beats as he eased his hold on her.

As he looked at her there was no doubt in her mind that he wasn't acting. He was Marc Renaud and he was as shattered as she was by what had happened. The door slammed again, and voices drifted to them from the side entrance of the cavernous sound stage. He lifted her to her feet, touched her arm with a sad, fleeting caress, and took the torn material of her dress in his hand. "Can it be fixed?"

Sasha found her voice. "There are safety pins in the makeup room," she said, blushing slightly. "I think I can patch it up."

He nodded and pointed to a smaller makeup room off the set. Sasha broke away from his gaze and turned to go, awkwardly, her heart pounding.

"Sasha—" He caught her by the arm and swung her around.

The silence exploded with what he was going to say, what he *didn't* say. His jaw flexed against the raw, dark emotion in his eyes, and finally, he exhaled. "You were brilliant," he said, his voice rough. "You're a natural actress. Do the scene half as well on camera, and it will be a masterpiece."

Acting? He thought she was acting? She stepped back and turned away as several members of the crew emerged boisterously out of the shadows.

Five

"Cut! Stop rolling!" Marc Renaud called to his camera operator. A stifled sigh of resignation echoed through the set as sound men, mixers, and prop people shifted position restively, adjusted equipment, and waited to do their director's bidding.

Sasha sagged out of Carlos's arms and sank back on her knees, too exhausted to ask Marc what was wrong now. It was going on a dozen times that he'd stopped them mid-scene since they started the actual filming, and her nerves were rubbed raw. Tears of frustration stung at her eyelids as she turned her head away briefly on the pretext of brushing hair from her eyes.

Carlos heaved a sigh, patted Sasha's shoulder in a show of support, and stared up at Marc. "What's the problem?" he asked, a faint accusation in the question.

"It's still not working." Marc's voice was low, barbed.

Sasha looked up at her director, confused by the shadowed intensity in his features. Whatever accounted for his dark disposition, he'd become increasingly moody with every take.

"Jesse, you're a wanted man—" Marc said the words impatiently, approaching them. "The pack is closing in for the kill. Lisa, you've just turned your back on *everything* you know and love. You're frightened of this man, of the passion he arouses, of what's going to come of all this insanity. Let me see the desperation. *Make me feel it.*"

Sasha's hands became fists in her lap. She wasn't giving him desperation? She'd given him everything she had in her, time and again. Her impromptu rehearsal with him had left her so unnerved, so defenseless, she literally had come apart in the first take with Carlos. She'd wept and agonized, the emotion coming from her very core, a depth of feeling she wouldn't have believed possible in front of a production crew. When Marc had insisted on additional takes, she'd thrown herself into them. She and Carlos had riveted the crew to silence with their emotional nakedness. *What did he want?*

"Let's try it again," Marc called, returning to the edge of the set. "Where we left off. In position."

Mustering strength, Sasha drew herself up, caught hold of Carlos's arm, and looked up at him. Her voice was hoarse with fatigue as she spoke the first line, her hands unsteady. She'd barely finished the sentence when Marc stopped her again. He raked a hand through his hair, stared at her a moment, and then quietly requested that she, Carlos, and the crew take a five-minute break.

Sasha sank down on the bed and watched nervously as Marc drew his camera operator and an assistant director aside for a conference. Marc shook his head several times, in obvious disagreement with the other two men, and finally he turned away from them. He seemed to be coming to a decision as his eyes flicked to Sasha. "That's it for today," he said, addressing only her. "You can go."

"Go? Go where?" She sprang up, unable to disguise the stunned hurt in her voice. "I know you're not satisfied with the scene," she said, "but at least let me try to get it right. I'm sure I can."

"The scene isn't ready to shoot," he explained with calculated patience, "and I can't justify holding up a fifty-man crew for any more rehearsal time. Bink will drive you back to the beach house."

Indignation crackled along the stripped wires of Sasha's nervous system. She tossed her hair back, her chest rising with a quick, tight breath. "That's not fair—"

Carlos caught hold of her hand from behind, startling her to silence. "Don't fight Renaud," he advised, *sotto voce*. "Do what he wants. I'll talk to him once you're gone."

Smoldering with fury, Sasha's gaze connected dead-on with Marc's eyes. "All right, *fine*," she blurted out at last, wincing at the tight squeeze of Carlos's hand. 'I'll go, but I'm doing it under protest."

A sound technician scrambled out of Sasha's way, dragging his equipment with him as she stalked off the set. By the time she reached the makeup room, she was in tears and nearly wild with frustration and confusion. The man was a monster! She'd opened herself like a wound in the scene with Carlos, and still it wasn't enough for him? She pulled off the shirtdress, slipped into her sweats, and threw her things together. What *did* he want?

Bink and the limo were waiting for her outside

the sound stage's main entrance when she stormed out. It wasn't until the beach house came into view that Sasha realized she couldn't go into that prison of a building. She needed some air, some breathing room, or she was going to explode. She tapped on the opaque window that separated her from Bink, and it rolled down with an ominous whoosh.

"Bink, there's somewhere else I'd like to go," she told him, "my health club."

He glanced in the rearview mirror and shook his head. "The boss said I was to shuttle you back and forth from the studio—and nowhere else."

"Well, fine," she said, "You'll shuttle me down to The Fitness Factor, and *then* you'll shuttle me back here. I only need an hour or so to speak to my manager."

"Sorry, no can do. I've got my orders. The boss—"

"Your boss can take a long walk off a short pier!" Sasha fell back in the seat, exasperated, and feeling very much like a six-year-old on the brink of a tantrum. She closed her eyes for a moment, calming herself. They hadn't invented the beach house that could hold Sasha McCleod. She would figure out a way to get where she wanted to go if she had to swipe a bicycle!

Moments later, as Bink helped her out of the limo and into the expansive garage with its stable of cars, the solution hit her.

The southbound 405 freeway was already thick with commuter traffic when Sasha gunned the classic 1968 Corvette Stingray up the on ramp. In her haste, she'd chosen the sports car because it looked to be the oldest and least expensive of Marc's impressive chorus line of luxury cars. But now, checking out the digital-display instrument panel and the switches, knobs, and levers on the in-car entertainment system, Sasha realized she'd miscalculated. This baby was souped up and streamlined. One touch of her toe to the gas pedal and she was at warp speed.

Yes, she had made a mistake. She had hot-wired a fully customized fantasy wagon. She had undoubtedly picked the most expensive car of the bunch!

By the time she reached The Fitness Factor, she'd calmed herself with the knowledge that she would be back at the beach house well before Marc arrived. He always worked late at the studio, sometimes well into the night. If she timed this excursion right, he would never know she was gone.

Sasha found T.C. right where she knew he would be, in the juice bar, gossiping with a sweet young thing in a shocking chartreuse leotard. His companion was the new aerobics instructor he'd hired, she reasoned, approaching their table.

"Compadre!" T.C. belted out, dodging as she playfully boxed him on the shoulder.

"Compadre?" Sasha puckered her brows in a mock frown. "When did you start calling me that?"

"When you put me in charge of this place." He winked and waved her into a chair at the table.

"Speaking of which," she said, nodding to his companion as she sat, "how are things going?"

"Magnifico." He shrugged immodestly. "What else? That studio mogul of yours sent down a CPA to get our books in order and streamline the accounting operation. I haven't had to do a lick of work since you left. By the way," he said, motioning toward his young companion, "this is Cindy, our new slave driver. She runs a mean aerobics class."

Flushing prettily, Cindy stood and excused herself. "I'm about to start the next session," she told Sasha. "Why don't you join us?"

T.C. grinned. "Shimmy into some skins and jump along."

Sasha immediately realized that was just what she needed, a good workout. It would clear her head, bring her back to earth. Maybe she could even make some sense of what had happened earlier. "Sure, be down in a minute," she said, nodding to the departing Cindy.

T.C. sobered as he stared at her. "What's wrong, boss? I can always tell when you're upset. Your earlobes swell up. Trouble in tinsel town?"

Sasha touched her ear, caught his droll grin, and avenged herself by stealing his glass of juice for a test sip. "You wouldn't believe the trouble," she admitted, deciding the fruity concoction had possibilities. "Umm, papaya-coconut?"

She proceeded to tell him about the dismal morning in detail, including her torrid rehearsal with Marc. T.C. had always functioned as a kid brother/father-confessor, the one person in Sasha's life she could pour her heart out to without fear of lectures or disapproval. And she knew T.C. would keep what she told him confidential.

"And then," she said, finishing the story, "when he couldn't get the button undone, *he ripped my dress.* Can you imagine?" She fell back in the chair and hooked her leg over the side. "Okay, so it *was* in the script, but who'd have thought he'd actually do it! What do you think, T.C.? Am I in over my head?"

Her office manager arched an eyebrow, then flexed an impressively toned bicep. "Say the word and I'll clean his clock."

Sasha smiled at his macho show of concern. It

was such a relief to be home. Such a relief to be with people who cared. "I'll keep that in mind." Remembering the sensation of Marc's fingers against her skin, she rolled her head back, gazed at the ceiling. "Actually, it was kind of thrilling in a prehistoric sort of way."

"Uh-oh," T.C. muttered, "you *are* in over your head. My advice is to get your sweat pants down to Cindy's aerobics class and work off that silly smile." He pointed a finger toward the stairway to the gym. "Git."

"Coming?" she asked, rising to take his advice.

He lifted his juice glass. "Soon as I finish off what little you've left me of this ambrosia."

The exercise class was everything Sasha had hoped. It was a thorough workout, and she didn't have time to think about anything but counting out beats. She was muscling through the last of fifty tummy curls when T.C. rolled up behind her.

"Sasha—"

"Not now, T.C.," she said with a gasp, hauling herself up and tucking her chin into her chest.

"Sasha, I think you'd better—"

"Ms. McCleod?"

Sasha bolted up to a sitting position and craned her head around in the direction of the angry male voice. Marc Renaud was standing in the doorway with an I-could-cheerfully-strangle-you-with-my-bare-hands glower on his face.

The entire class halted to get a look at him.

"What are you doing here?" There was accusation in Sasha's voice as she sprang to her feet. "You followed me?"

"Call me impetuous," Marc said angrily, "but I always follow women who steal my car."

"I didn't steal it, I borrowed it."

"You and I need to talk, McCleod." To the amazement of all assembled, he strode over, took her by the arm, and escorted her right out of the gym.

T.C. wheeled out into the hallway right behind them. Sizing Marc up with a glance, he inquired bluntly of Sasha, "What's the word? Do I flatten this guy under my tires?"

"What a lovely idea," Sasha muttered. "Perhaps another time, T.C. Mr. Renaud and I have some things to settle."

"Yeah, well, I'll just stick around," T.C. declared.

"It's okay, really. I'll be all right." Sasha's voice had a note of insistence, but her office manager didn't budge.

Marc folded his arms and proceeded to rub his jaw, an easy gesture, but not quite casual enough to hide his strategizing gaze. Apparently he was trying to decide how best to deal with Sasha's bodyguard on wheels. "T.C.," he said finally, "can we talk? Man-to-man?"

T.C. shrugged, glancing at Sasha for her approval. "Yeah, I guess so. Why not?"

Sasha watched as the two men conversed between themselves for all of two minutes. The exchange ended quickly and painlessly with T.C. shooting Sasha an I-kinda-like-this-guy grin and wheeling off.

"How did you do that?" Sasha asked as Marc returned.

"I can be charming when I have to. Actually I offered him the unlimited use of my little black book."

"I see."

"And I cemented the deal by promising not to do you bodily harm." The smile he produced was a little slow in coming, but roguishly engaging once it arrived. "I won't, either. Not quite yet anyway," he amended under his breath.

Sasha tossed her hair, refusing to smile back at him. He had his nerve, enlisting the help of her office manager! "What do you want?"

"What do I *want*? That's got to be the rhetorical question of the century. I want to know why you stole my car, why you violated our agreement and left the beach house unescorted."

"I had a bad day." Sarcasm tingled in her throat. "There was this French movie director who kissed me dizzy and—" She caught her breath, suddenly aware of the change in his eyes, the dark sparkle in their depths.

"Yeah, I had one of those days too," he said.

Sasha found herself staring at him, struck by something she couldn't put a name to. The dramatic shadings in his face and the subtle nuances of mood and emotion fascinated her. He was like an abstract painting, the meaning of which she couldn't decipher but which she couldn't look away from.

"Then perhaps you can understand why I'm upset," she said at last, gradually aware that it was the sensuality knit into the curve of his smile that was making her stomach knot.

"Sure I understand," he said. "That's why I'm here. To talk about it."

"Not to get your car?"

"*And* to get my car."

He let the silence linger a moment, then caught hold of her wrist, startling her heart into near failure.

"I'd like you to come back with me," he said.

The words were quietly spoken, but Sasha felt their power. His smile, superficially casual, had an energy that slipped past her thoughts and spoke to her emotions.

"There's something I want to show you at the

studio," he added mysteriously. "Bink is waiting outside. He'll drive the limo back and we'll take the Corvette."

Sasha's protest was halted by an indrawn breath as his fingers pressed into the sensitive flesh of her inner wrist and a spark of sensuality flared in his eyes.

"Sasha, it's important."

Her heart was hammering, her curiosity piqued. Timing *is* everything, she thought to herself, and this man had an infallible instinct for it. There was no way she could say no. "I'll get my purse."

Their trip back to the studio proceeded in silence while Marc battled the rigors of rush-hour traffic. Several times Sasha was on the brink of bringing up the incident from earlier that morning, but there didn't seem to be any polite way to ask a man what all the rage and passion in his eyes had been about.

As for his dismissing her from the set, though it was an easier subject to broach, she wasn't sure she wanted to know why he'd done it. He was so pointedly silent, she'd half begun to wonder if he was taking her back to present her with her walking papers. More than likely, she told herself, it was going to be another coaching session, complete with lectures on giving herself over to the character. If there was to be any more kissing involved, she thought ironically, glancing at him, she wanted hazardous-duty pay.

The studio was dark and deserted when they drove up an hour and a half later. "What are we doing here now, Marc?" Sasha asked, glancing around the ten-acre lot, only absently aware that she'd never called him by his first name before.

"All will become clear in a minute." He slammed the car door and came around to help her out. "Come on," he said, taking her by the hand.

He led her into a small projection room, deposited her in a cushioned seat in the middle row of the theater, and went back to the booth to rewind the film. Finally the lights went down and the footage they'd shot that morning began to run. A moment later he joined her.

Uncomfortably aware that it was her director next to her, Sasha watched the scene with Carlos unfold before her eyes. At first she resisted the experience, distancing herself emotionally, but gradually the performances began to compel her in ways she didn't fully comprehend. Before it was over, she had compressed her hands into a ball against her stomach, and there were tears in her eyes. The scene's tension was palpable. Its emotion had left her shaking—Jesse's rage, Lisa's agony, their desperate passion.

"It's good, isn't it?" Marc stated quietly, not looking at her.

"Yes, but I thought—"

"I was wrong."

"What?" Sasha watched him rise, turn on the lights, and disappear into the booth to shut off the projector. He was back in the aisle, waiting for her, shortly afterward.

"As soon as I saw the dailies, I knew I'd made a mistake," he said, his shrugged shoulder and upswept hand a very European gesture of contrition.

"About me? I was good, then?"

He stared at her from halfway across the room and gazed at her for a very long time. "You weren't good," he said, "you were stunning. I don't know why I didn't see it before. You have the quality of an opal that has to be held in a certain light to see the fire." He pointed to the large silver rectangle in front of them. "That screen is your light. Your fire comes through."

Sasha released a breath and felt the warm air shaking in her throat. She was laughing, trembling from the impact of his compliment. She'd had no idea how much it would mean to her. For one fleetingly emotional moment she recalled the eight-year-old girl who'd taken the blue ribbon at an intramural track meet. That serious, amber-eyed child had worked most of her young life for the scraps of her stern father's praise, and had finally, unexpectedly, received a pat on the head.

"I thought I could infuse some energy into the original by editing it with cuts of your scene," he went on. "But I'm not going to bother with that now. This scene is too good not to use. Lord—" He laughed almost bitterly. "It's the best damn scene in the movie."

He walked to her and took hold of her wrist. His grip was casual, but it was too proprietary a gesture to be dismissed.

"I know what you need," he said.

A quick curl of excitement whorled in the pit of her stomach. *I'll just bet you do,* she thought, wondering if she had either the will or the strength to resist him. Every nerve and fiber of her body resonated to his closeness. If he wanted to ravish her there, on the projection room floor, she would undoubtedly surrender without a whimper.

A faint twinkle telegraphed his intentions. "You need some rest," he said.

"Rest?" It was a simple enough concept, but its literal meaning eluded her for a moment. "As in shut-eye?" She was completely unprepared for the friendly warmth in his smile.

He laughed, nodded. "Tomorrow's another rough day," he reminded her. "We've got some location shooting scheduled down in Newport Beach, running and swimming shots. You're going to need your strength."

Sasha's face must have fallen, because he stopped and studied her, his brows lifting. "Something wrong?"

Only her expectations, she thought, shaking her head. "What could be wrong? A girl can always use a good night's sleep, right?"

The new moon floated restlessly through cloud cover, highlighting drifts, transforming them into meringue desserts ladeled into the shiny black bowl of the sky. It was a luminous night, unseasonably warm and muggy for January, and Marc Renaud couldn't sleep.

He pulled a couple of pillows behind him and sat up, leaning his head against the kingsize bed's bamboo headboard. A pack of cigarettes, a bottle of Courvoisier, and a balloon glass of the expensive cognac languished on the night table beside the bed. He'd considered all three several times, and had abstained. He wasn't sure why exactly, but he suspected it had something to do with Sasha's sermonizing. It struck him as ironic that a woman might still have that kind of civilizing effect on a man, even in the eighties.

She sure as hell was the reason for his insomnia.

He draped one arm along the back of the headboard and stared at the ceiling, remembering what had happened to his composure when he'd first seen the rushes of her scene with Carlos. A tiny bomb had exploded in his chest—and in his brain. He'd reviewed the footage more out of curiosity than from any expectation of being able to use it. And yet from the first frame he'd been rocked by what he saw. She burned up the screen, a woman possessed and yet terrified of where her passions were taking her. She *was* Lisa. Why hadn't he seen that on the set?

The answer that came to him confirmed what he already feared—he couldn't trust himself to be objective where she was concerned. Maybe he hadn't wanted to let himself believe she could respond to Carlos the way she had to him. Because if he believed that, it would force him to admit she might have been acting, that the trembling passion had come from the actress, not the woman.

He glanced at the pack of Gauloises, the urge too strong to ignore this time. Tapping one out, he lit it and let the smoke curl up in front of his eyes. Aware of the cigarette's shape, its texture in his mouth, he took a long, slow drag and watched the embers flare to crimson, the paper curl back. Its slow, smoldering fire made him think of her.

His body responded to the image, to its uncoiling sensuality. Heat warmed his throat and brought a tightening pleasure to the base of his jaw. He blew a smoke ring and let it fade, watching its contours form the soft, misty curves of a woman's body. Crazy, he thought, he was seeing things the way he used to years ago, when he was still driven by passion rather than by obsession. His mind was alive with vivid impressions. He could feel her skin in the cool sheets that draped his lower torso. He could see her fire in the gold streams running through the cognac.

His next smoke ring drifted into the shape of the lush, supplicant fullness of a woman's breast. It shook slightly in some hidden air current, and the movement drove Marc's thoughts back to his own sweet pain when he'd ripped her dress earlier and felt her delicate flesh beneath his fingers. A sparkle of electricity awakened the nerves of his palm.

His body wanted to take him further. The current of pleasure in his groin demanded he replay it all in his mind . . . her reaction when he'd cupped her breast, the way she'd gasped and then arched back as the fire took her, thrusting herself into his hands. The act had enflamed him beyond belief.

He could feel himself hardening with the automatic surge of blood to his loins. She was down the hall, his body told him. A few doors away, lush and warm, scented with sleep and dreamy sensuality. Within seconds the blood was beating in every nerve center of his body, in his hands, in the cords of his neck, even in the soles of his feet. The hard throb in his groin reminded him that fantasy had its price.

He sucked in a breath, flicked on the light, and reached for the glass. Deep muscles clenched in protest as he drank the fiery brandy down and invoked the mythical willpower of the gods. *They must needs go whom the Devil drives*, he thought, remembering Cervantes's warning.

It was a half hour and several splashes of brandy later before he'd restored himself to something near normalcy. The power of his obsession was forcing him to come to grips with the situation, to look at it with the ruthless practicality he applied to everything else in life. Sasha McCleod was a mercurial and desirable woman. She also had a backbone of reinforced steel and a hammerlock on her emotions, but when she let her guard down, she was a natural actress. He hadn't exaggerated. She was stunning on film, and there was no doubt in his mind that, if handled correctly, she could save his movie. That was why he had to get his priorities straight. He would have to do without the woman because his movie *couldn't* do without the actress.

He thought about her well into the night, about how she had reignited something in him. She was like a power surge, a current fueling him with energy. She had revitalized him and stoked the fire in his belly. Even the film had become important to him again, and for personal reasons rather than for professional ones. He wanted it to be good, not because it was his comeback picture or for the recognition it could bring, but because it was about the agony of choice, the ongoing pain of life and relationships. It was about people, *about him*.

His brain percolated with ideas for new scenes he could use her in. Energized, he smoked constantly and worked at the bottle of cognac, finishing off half of it before he could slow his racing thoughts.

Hours later, relaxing into the pillows, he closed his eyes and waited for sleep. When it came it was surprisingly deep and restful, devoid of dreams, a kind of calm preceding the storm. Without moving, barely breathing, he drifted in a cocoonlike state, no more aware of coming danger than the butterfly pupa is of chrysalis.

As the first light of dawn was breaking on the horizon, the deafening crack of a thunderbolt brought him out of the strange tranquility. He jackknifed up, a scream locked in the taut muscles of his gut. Lightning flashed outside, illuminating the wall of windows with quick bright bursts.

Sweat broke out on his forehead as the splitting thunder and the crackling white light conjured up horrors from the past. *An old man, his abundant white hair askew, his rheumy eyes sharp with hate . . . the flashing metal of a gun barrel, the crack of its report . . . and then the screams, the piercing, life-shattering screams.*

Marc threw off the sheet, strode to the glass doors, and flung them open. He stared out at the sluggish ocean, up at the roiling heavens. As though on cue, the thunderheads split open and the rains began. It was surreal and beautiful, a storm ordered up by a special-effects unit.

His gut was tight with sadness and ancient rage.

His eyes were moist with tears.

Wearing only pajama bottoms, he walked into the torrential downburst, letting it drench his body and pommel the hellish memories away. A racking shudder took him as the cool rain pounded against his face.

That night of screams and gunshots had changed Marc's life forever. It was the night he had surrendered his last illusion. It was the night he had made a promise to himself never to feel anything again.

Six

Wearing only her white eyelet nightgown, Sasha sat in the alcove of her bedroom and watched the horizon flash on and off with blinding light. A thunderstorm at dawn, she thought, what an eerie way to start the day. She'd been up most of the night, too excited and nervous to sleep. Wired, T.C. called it. Sasha smiled. If she was any more wired, they could string her between telephone poles.

It frightened her a little to be so exuberant. She was still high as Everest from seeing the dailies—and from the compliments Marc had paid her. Stunning, he'd said, a fire opal.

She rose and walked to the windows as the low storm clouds broke open and a monsoonlike downpour began. Dense with rain, the sky was oyster-gray and beautiful. She wondered briefly if the cloudburst would affect their location shooting, but the prospect of a delay didn't bother her. Nothing could have bothered her at present, she suspected. Besides, the weather matched her mood, dramatic and expectant.

Drawn to the storm, she walked to the patio door and opened it, listening to the rain clatter on the wooden awning overhead. The lightning struck again, illuminating the coastline as she stepped outside and scanned up and down the beach, taking in the splendor. It was only when she swung around to look at the hills that she noticed him.

Marc Renaud stood on the deck off his bedroom thirty feet to the west of her. Startled, Sasha caught hold of the railing to steady herself. For a moment she wasn't sure if he was a man or an apparition. The sight of him poised in the cloudburst, his arms at his sides, his head thrown back as the rain washed over him, was as staggering as it was unexpected. Water glistened in his dark hair, streamed down his chest, and plastered his thin pajama pants to his body. In the translucent light of dawn he looked mythic and mystical, a pagan god in a fertility ritual.

Lightning split the sky again just above his head, and Sasha flinched back with a reaction near to awe.

Certain that she must be eavesdropping on some private moment, Sasha stepped backed into her room. Her sense of bewilderment grew as she tried to make sense of what she'd seen. What had possessed him to do such a thing? For some reason, the emotion in his eyes during their love scene came back to her, the pain, the pinprick of rage. She wondered again what he'd done. Or what someone had done to him.

Even in the quieter moments they'd had together, which had been too few, there'd been a melancholy unease about Marc Renaud. Her mind jumped automatically to the possibility that disturbed her most—that his turmoil had something to do with Leslie. Had she left him? Was Leslie the source of his conflict?

Sasha walked to her still-made bed and sank down, dropping back onto the pillow. Lost in thought, she tugged absently at her lower lip, a holdover habit from childhood moments of deep contemplation. It disturbed her terribly to think of him racked with pain over another woman. No, worse, it hurt like hell. Why in the world it should affect her so intensely, she didn't know, but there was a viselike ache around her heart that felt hot and tender as a new bruise. It was almost as though something precious had been taken from her.

The sensation was pervasive and astonishingly painful, and it was alleviated only a little as she pressed her hand to her chest. It was like an arrow through the heart. Oh, she was being ridiculous, she told herself, shaking her head as she sat up and swung her legs off the bed. A person had to be in love to have a broken heart, and she couldn't be in love with a man she'd known for only a week, a moody character she wasn't even sure she liked very much.

She walked to the patio door again and touched the glass, watching the rain. She didn't step out to see if he was still there. The storm was lessening, and somehow she knew he wouldn't be.

By the time dawn had turned into morning, she had brought her situation into focus. She was suffering from a bad case of infatuation. If she cared to probe, she probably would find that it all stemmed back to some unresolved adolescent crush—the high school science teacher who'd failed to notice her, maybe. It wasn't hero worship exactly, but it was close. It was understandable, even appropriate. Marc was a famous director and arguably the most attractive man she'd ever met. If she didn't count his moods, there was plenty to be infatuated about.

An hour later, after an intense session of isometrics and a round of hot and cold showers—a relaxation trick Sasha had picked up from the colonel—she felt as though her sense of direction had been restored. Her murky feelings about Marc had been temporarily sidelined in favor of a weightier matter—his past relationship with Leslie. There were too many pieces missing to make a complete picture of the twosome. Sasha wanted to know exactly what had happened to his former star and live-in companion. Where was Leslie now? How did Marc feel about her?

The tantalizing smell of fresh-ground coffee wafted up the stairway as she descended to the first floor a short time later. Aware of the house's quiet, she made her way through the maze of hallways to the kitchen. For security reasons, the staff had all been dismissed except for Bink and Arturo, but neither was in evidence that morning.

Marc was standing at the kitchen window when Sasha entered. Unaware of her, he stared out at the gray sky, a cup of coffee in his hand, a French cigarette drooping seductively from his lips. His jeans, faded and glove-soft from wear, hugged his hips and defined his thighs and calves with the precision of an artist's brush. His chambray shirt was rolled up to the elbows and open at the neck.

Très continental, Sasha thought, hesitating in the doorway. He looked like he had been strolling on the Champs-Élysées and was transported magically into the kitchen. He also looked, well, decadent. She resisted the urge to take issue with the cigarette. If he wanted to ruin his lungs—and his life in the process—she told herself firmly, that was his prerogative.

"Hi," she said in a neutral tone. "Looks like we're in for some foul weather, doesn't it?" Humming quietly, she walked to the coffeemaker and poured herself a mugful. "How's this downpour going to affect the beach shoot?"

He took the cigarette out of his mouth with his thumb and forefinger, Bogart style, then tapped its ashes into the potted palm next to him and glanced over his shoulder at her. "We're shut down until the storm breaks. Pray for sunshine."

"I will," she said, debating the wisdom of joining him at the window. He didn't look as if he'd bite, though she suspected he might. The man certainly had a bizarre effect on her. She'd begun to feel slightly delirious with some of the random thoughts and notions that popped into her head where he was concerned. Just being around him was an event. She never knew quite what *she* was going to say or do next. Was that what made him a good director, she wondered. His ability to draw on the spontaneous, his ability to make people react instead of "act"?

When she finally did join him at the window, he drew himself out of his reflections long enough to nod at her and step back to the tiled counter to stub out his cigarette in an ashtray. His eyes were pale and intense, even at this hour of the morning, and they never quite seemed to leave her, even when he looked away.

She glanced out at the ocean uneasily, certain that it wasn't just his concern about the movie schedule that had him so pensive. It must have something to do with whatever had taken him out onto the deck in the rain.

"Paul said these delays cost tens of thousands of dollars daily."

"Paul was right for once," Marc answered.

Sasha cordoned off the rest of the questions lining up in her mind. This wasn't the time, she told herself. His body might be in the kitchen, but his psyche was still out in the rain. As he studied the coastline, she studied his profile, more curious about him than ever. Like Faust, she would have made a bargain with the devil at that moment to know what he was thinking.

It wasn't the movie on Marc's mind *or* the haunting memory of that night long ago that had forced him out into the storm. It was Sasha. He might have looked preoccupied when she'd entered, but he hadn't missed how appealing she was in her jeans and brief cotton top, her blond hair cascading around her. He hadn't missed the fact that she wasn't wearing a bra. Her ample breasts shimmied under the tank top when she moved, straining at the fabric in ways that made his thoughts steam up like a teenager's car window and his hands ache with adult male urges.

"You're staring at me," she pointed out.

"Staring? Was I? Sorry, I've got things on my mind." He smiled faintly, aware that what was on his mind would have shocked the hell out of her. His body was quickening, responding to her physically, but his mind had taken a different tack, looped back on itself and gone inward. He was thinking about himself, about the dark spot in his soul. Strange as it sounded, he sensed that she had something he needed badly, and suddenly he'd begun having crazy thoughts . . . about her stubborn purity of mind and spirit, about the white flame that burned inside her—about sex with her . . . or making love to her. Which would it be? He didn't know, but he did know it would be incendiary and consuming. He did know the fantasy of taking her to bed obsessed him like danger obsesses the thrillseeker.

He pulled a pack of cigarettes from his breast pocket, lit one, and inhaled deeply. Why did he imagine that her fire could cauterize whatever it touched? Why did he believe she could burn him clean?

"Marc?"

She touched his arm and he turned away, staring out to sea, pulling deeply on the cigarette. A cinchlike sensation pressed hard around his heart. It wasn't pain, he decided. He barely remembered what pain felt like . . . until now, until her.

When he turned back, she was across the room, pouring herself another cup of coffee and looking as though she'd picked up on his mental impulses. She stared at him uneasily, her eyes large. Neither of them spoke, and in the quiet that expanded around them, the words left unsaid seemed to take on tremendous import.

Finally her searching gaze flicked to his cigarette, and a frown of disapproval surfaced. He knew damn well it wasn't his smoking that was bothering her, but at least it was a safer topic than anything he could come up with.

"This isn't personal, okay?" he said, taking one last deep drag before he stubbed out the cigarette. "I'm not out to sabotage your one-woman campaign to rid the world of ashtrays. I'm addicted. It has nothing to do with you."

She pressed both hands around the coffee cup and took a drink with steadying slowness. "Thirteen years off your life just like that," she said, her voice faint but firm. She was a woman who held to her convictions, even under siege.

"The good die young," he reminded her.

"Umm, but it's not a fun way to go. The lungs turn black and gummy with corrosion," she said, "the heart valves clog up with fat—"

"Enough." He pulled the entire pack from his pocket and crushed it. "If I live to be a hundred, it's your fault."

They stared at each other, and at last she smiled.

He nodded. An unspoken truce was in the making.

"If you're really thinking of quitting," Sasha offered, perhaps a little too eagerly, "I've got a few tips. You have to learn to respect yourself, of course, and your body. Anticipate success—that's a must—practice deep breathing, and when you get the urge—" she shrugged and smiled as though it were so so simple—"do something else."

His grin deepened. "I've got the urge."

Sasha caught the sexy flash of blue in his eyes and felt the nape of her neck tingle. Boy, who doesn't, she thought. "Can I suggest some . . . exercise?"

"Suggest away."

"Stretching exercises, maybe some isometrics?"

"Actually, I was thinking about—"

"No," she said flatly, anticipating him, "no pushups. You need something calming and meditative, like yoga. I could show you a couple of postures."

"I wish you would."

Moments later they were out on the deck off the kitchen and she was demonstrating some basic yoga positions. She knew he was putting her on at first, but the enthusiasm of her presentation gradually won him over, and by the time she got around to explaining the benefits of deep breathing, he seemed sincerely interested. She even coaxed him into a cobra position, which she promised him was yoga's answer to the pushup.

"Relax and raise your upper torso until you're at a forty-five-degree angle with the floor. Yes . . . there . . . good! How does that feel?"

His groan was rich with laughter. "It feels like I'm going to need a chiropractor."

As they lay on the floor afterward, Marc with his arms crossed under his head, contemplating the ceiling, Sasha propped up on her elbow, contemplating him, she realized it was the closest he'd ever been to being in a congenial mood. It pleased her to think that she might have had something to do with it.

They talked casually about yoga, about *Tell Me No Lies*, and finally she broached one of the questions that had been heavy on her mind. "Paul told me that Leslie was indisposed," she said cautiously. "I hope she's not seriously ill?"

He rose to a sitting position, worked a catch out of his shoulder muscle, and roped his arms around his legs. "Paul was being discreet," he replied bluntly. "The truth is, Leslie wasn't happy with the arrangement that she and I had."

Arrangement? A pregnant word if ever Sasha had heard one. Struck by its implications, and by his totally unexpected openness, she sat up too. Now we're getting somewhere, she thought, barely able to rein in her curiosity. "You mean business, of course."

"No, I mean personal. She walked off the set because I called off our engagement."

"Engagement? You were engaged?" Suddenly Sasha's heart was pounding like a jackhammer. This was more information than she'd counted on, perhaps even wanted. "Then you must have been in love . . . very much in love, both of you, with each other?"

He stared at her over a hunched shoulder, irony in his expression. "Only one of us was very much in love," he said, "and that was Leslie—with her makeup mirror."

"Oh, I see." Sasha sagged back down to her elbow, literally weak with relief.

They were both quiet for the next few moments, Sasha trying to assimilate the land mines of information she'd tripped over in the last seconds, Marc wondering what she was going to come up with next. She'd been thrown by his directness, that was obvious, but he may also have inadvertently whet her appetite by his willingness to talk about forbidden subjects. He suspected he had. She didn't disappoint him.

"If you didn't love her," she asked, a thoughtful naïveté in her voice, "then why did you become engaged to her?"

The ensuing silence accentuated every sound in the room, the soft whir of the dehumidifier in the corner, the precise tick tick tick of the wall clock. "It seemed like the thing to do at the time," he said finally.

"Where is she now?"

Marc pushed to his feet. His reticence had nothing to do with Leslie. His mistake, he realized, was in opening himself up to Sasha's questions in the first place. She was fatally inquisitive, a woman who wouldn't give up until she'd pared to the bone, until she knew everything. By his openness, he'd given her tacit permission to continue probing into whatever inspired her next—his life, his past.

White-capped breakers crashed on the beach as he walked to the railing and stared out. He knew exactly how it would go once she'd discovered the grisly truth. She would either shrink away or feel compelled to save him. Yes, he thought, she had "cause" written all over her. She held a better, brighter view of the world that included rescuing lost souls and fixing broken lives. Well, he wasn't lost. He knew exactly where he was—in hell, a fiery abyss of his own making. At least he had an edge over ninety percent of the human race who didn't have a clue where they were.

"Leslie didn't leave a forwarding address," he said, aware that she probably wouldn't believe it. "And I don't appreciate or need the second-rate psychoanalysis."

"Second-rate what?" She looked stung and confused.

"That respect-yourself crap, the deep breathing, the yoga. Save it for wishful thinkers week."

"I was only trying to—"

"Help? You want to help, Sasha?" He deliberately sliced through her good intentions with his voice. "In the future, learn your lines and mind your own business."

She sprang to her feet, her eyes flashing. "Yes, as a matter of fact, I did want to help. So sue me! I've been trying to get to know you. Marc Renaud the man, the human being. All right, call me a bleeding heart, but I thought it was pain I saw in your eyes yesterday. Now I know it was pure meanness. You're not a lost soul"—her voice rose with what was now painfully obvious to her—"you're a bastard."

She grabbed up her sneakers, stormed down the steps and onto the beach, her hair flying in the wind. The rain had stopped, replaced by a misty drizzle. Watching her slog barefoot through the wet sand to the water, Marc felt a mix of emotions. Lord, but she was a spitfire. He loved that about her, but he also knew it left them with about as much chance of a relationship as the Christians and the lions. They were both too strong-willed and volatile to be together for long without clashing.

Walking to the steps, he followed her with his gaze as she disappeared down the coastline, running gracefully at the water's edge. She ran like a marathoner, gliding with an economy of movement that was surprisingly sensual. Her legs were curves of gold in the waning sunlight.

Unbidden, an image took him by storm. He could almost see her, feel her beneath him, moaning and supine as he sheathed himself in the melting warmth between those legs. He wanted to follow her. He caught hold of the doorjamb, his jaw flexed against the sweet, stinging riot of desire in his muscles.

The drizzly mist penetrated Sasha's clothing as she ran, but it didn't cool her simmering temper. If she was angry at him, then she was furious at herself. How could she have been so naïve. The man had a cruel streak. It was there for all the world to see, and she'd insisted on labeling it pain, sadness? She wasn't naïve. She was a thirty-year-old sap!

She pressed on at a faster-than-normal gait, as if by running hard she could burn away indignation like a car engine sloughs off carbon. The impact of the hard sand reverberated through her body and blurred the horizon into an unbroken seascape of gunmetal-gray water and sky.

Her heart stilled as she picked up something other than her own rhythmic footfall, a soft thudding sound that came from behind. She glanced over her shoulder and saw him twenty yards back, striding steadily after her. He was shirtless, faded jeans his only clothing.

He's following me, she realized, accelerating the pace. A muscle in her calf twitched, threatening to cramp as she pushed herself harder, beyond the limits of her normal endurance. Moments later she glanced over her shoulder again. He was still back there—and moving up on her with every stride. He wasn't following her, he was chasing her! She began to sprint, her breath coming in hard, painful spurts.

A wave thundered up onto the beach, catching her legs and dragging her off course as it rolled back to sea. Her imagination rocketed out of control as she glanced back again and saw him closing the distance between them. Her nerves and muscles jumped, galvanized by a primal shriek, the instinctive fear of pursuit. She gulped in a breath, thrashing through the foam. When she hit the hard-packed sand, she dug in, running as though her survival depended on it. With every cell in her body she fought to outdistance him.

A driftwood branch snapped under her foot. Thinking it was him behind her, she imagined him catching her, his hands on her arms, his body against hers. The vision sent thrills of apprehension through her. She flew over the sand with frantic, mindless precision. *No, she would never let him catch her, never let him take her that way.*

Marc came up behind her. A little more than three yards back now, he'd been narrowing the gap between them steadily. His breathing was deep and fast, and the feverish heat of the chase was in his blood. He was going to catch her, by God, if it was the last thing he did.

Another yard or so and he could tag her. A flying leap and a hand hooked around her ankle, and he would send them both sprawling in the sand. The idea had a certain sophomoric appeal— warm bodies rolling and tumbling every which way—but the consequences didn't. She already was furious and he liked living. Better that he outrun her and then gently, *very* gently, cut her off at the pass.

He mobilized his energy for the capture. She was still running expertly, showing no obvious signs of fading, but then, she was a trained runner. *Hell, she didn't smoke.* His ace in the hole, he reminded himself, was speed. He was fast, a strong finisher with a kick. He considered her smoothly striding form and smiled. She didn't stand a chance. Sixty seconds and she's mine, he thought, breaking into a sprint.

As though sensing his plan, she cut out, too, and they raced across the beach like bandits, re-designing the drifting sand dunes with the light skim of their footfall. Sixty seconds was a slight underestimation on Marc's part. She was invincible, barely touching the ground by the time he caught her. Gasping for air, he ran her off the shoreline and into the water. "Slow down, dammit," he ordered, latching on to her arm.

Off balance, she floundered farther into the frigid, knee-deep surf, nearly dumping them both in the drink. "Let go of me!" she said, obviously in a perfect fury. With a mighty tug she wrested free and promptly began kicking water at him.

"Hold it, hold it!" He braved her flashing feet to grab her by the wrists and tug her toward him. She never stopped flailing, even when he jerked her so close their mouths were just inches apart. "I wanted to apologize," he said, breathing in air that was hot from her lungs. "What does that make me? A mass murderer in your book?" He jumped back, dodging her shot at his shin. "Hey! Take it easy, I'm sorry—"

"Oh, now you're *sorry*?" She ceased struggling for a moment, her chest heaving. "My goodness, what prompted this? Afraid I'll walk off your picture the way Leslie did? I'm beginning to feel a real kinship with that woman."

"All right, then," he said, releasing her, "no apologies. Can I run back with you at least?"

"I don't know, can you?"

It was a good question. They were at least four miles from the beach house, and after chasing her for several minutes and nearly *not* catching her, Marc was hardly in the mood to admit that his legs were giving out on him. "Try me," he said, challenging her. He broke into a trot and wheeled around, running backward. "Maybe I should run this way to even things up?"

"Show-off," she said with a disdainful arch of her eyebrow.

He spun, started off down the beach, and a moment later she was right beside him, running like a perpetual motion machine. He set a fast pace and held it, but she strode alongside him easily.

By the time they'd completed their second mile, Marc was running out of steam, but he was thoroughly intrigued. She barely seemed to be breathing beyond the soft shiver of her breasts beneath her tank top. She was so quiet, he could have sworn she was in a trance. When he remarked on her silence, she said simply, "I'm minding my own business. That's what you wanted, isn't it?"

Spoken like a forties movie heroine, he thought, smiling to himself. *I've got one tough dame on my hands.*

Marc's legs were cramping by the third mile, and his lungs were screaming for air, but he wasn't about to slow up. Not with her gliding beside him like a winged messenger of the gods. Summoning reserves of energy, he dug in and labored along until he'd caught his second wind.

By the time the beach house came into view, a distant rectangle on the horizon, he was moving with relative ease and beginning to feel a little cocky. "First one to the stairs takes the trophy," he challenged her, referring to the stairway that led from the beach to the house.

She glanced over at him, smiled wickedly, and nodded. They both broke into a sprint at once. "What sort of trophy?" she called after him as he pulled into the lead.

"I'll tell you when you lose it," he yelled back.

The remaining half mile was the race of Marc's life. His ego was fully involved now. He wanted to win, dammit—for himself, for posterity, for all the men whose cigarettes she had snapped in half. He glanced back, saw she was on his heels, and shifted into high gear. He thought his lungs would burst as he fought to hold his lead. His legs felt like weights, and his heart was a roaring monster in his ears. The stairway came into view, and he threw up a fist in triumph.

"Marc!" Sasha cried from just behind him.

He jerked his head around, but she wasn't there. Had something happened to her? Where was she? He swung around the other way and grunted, hurtling forward as his toe caught on something. He hit the ground on his hands and knees and somersaulted with the furious momentum of his driving pace. His muscles absorbed the wet, hard-ridged sand like body blows. Unable to stop himself, he rolled right into the surf, howling as an icy wave washed over him.

Hearing Sasha's squeal of glee, he rolled over and watched her dash up the stairs. In the moment it took him to figure out what was going on, another wave broke over him. He hadn't snagged his foot on a rock. She'd tripped him!

Following her flight as she disappeared into the house, he made a silent promise to himself. That golden-haired hellion had to be taught a lesson!

Seven

Alone in her room, Sasha stripped off her damp tank top, jeans, and panties, and wrapped herself in a big fluffy towel. Her heart was still beating at a rapid pace and her body was glistening with perspiration, but she didn't feel a bit tired. Quite the opposite, she was exhilarated.

Glancing at her reflection in the bathroom's wall of mirrors, she saw the reckless twinkle in her eye and felt a flash of guilt. Laughter bubbled in her throat. Lord, but it had felt wonderful to have the last laugh on Marc Renaud. Luckily the water had broken his fall, she thought, stifling a giggle.

Enjoying herself thoroughly, she pulled her hair up into a loose chignon and began pinning the abundant golden mass into place. It was only as one of her dad's stock sayings came to mind that the thought of consequences interrupted her muffled glee. *Never laugh at live dragons.*

"Uh-oh," she murmured, halting in the act of securing her topknot, "if ever there was a live dragon."

The sound of Marc's wail echoed in her ears, raising goose bumps on her arms. He was going to kill her, of course. He would string her up by her ankles, stretch her on the rack, or try something uniquely French. The guillotine? The only smart move was to stay away from him until he cooled down. What had possessed her?

She congratulated herself on remembering to lock the bedroom door as she dropped the towel and stepped into the shower stall. Not that she really believed he would violate her privacy by storming into her room uninvited, but still, a girl couldn't be too careful.

Turning slowly in the jet spray, she let the steaming water pelt her body and relax her taut muscles and nerves. Later, soaping herself down with one of the fragrant, lavender-scented bars she found heaped in a procelain shell, she allowed her mind to drift to an image of Marc Renaud coming up behind her, chasing her. A soft thrill formed in the pit of her stomach. It swirled like a feather in a spring breeze as she imagined him catching hold of her wrists and tugging her toward him. *He'd come to apologize?* Lord, but he was unpredictable and magnetic, a lightning rod to her senses.

Such a difficult, complicated man, she thought, holding up her hair to rinse the soap from her neck and shoulders. Would she ever find out what made him tick? She wasn't even sure it was safe to try. He had a countdown tension about him that made her think of a delayed-action bomb. And yet there were other qualities about him that captivated her—the misty sadness, the piercing intelligence. . . . He was such a beguiling man with those crystalline eyes of his, that heartbreaking mouth. "Who are you, Marc Renaud?" she asked, a sigh slipping into the question.

She was still in a reflective mood as she stepped out of the shower, rewrapped herself with the fat blue towel, and entered the bedroom. How was she going to while away the rest of the day in the confines of this room, she wondered, opening the lingerie drawer of her dresser.

Black, white, or champagne, she mused, fingering through a neat stack of lacy panties. As the scent of patchouli wafted up to her nose, she realized Arturo didn't just fold well. He'd tucked a sachet in the drawer somewhere. Delighted, she picked out a pair of champagne panties and hesitated, thinking she'd heard something. Yes . . . there. She heard it again, a soft clicking sound. "Oh Lord, no—" she said with a gasp, whirling as a key turned in the lock and the door swung open.

Eclipsing the streaming light from the hallway, Marc paused long enough to take stock of her. His jeans were still damp, his face still flushed from the run—or from anger. It was hard to tell which, except that he was angry. He was massaging a knot on his forearm, and the muscles that ran from his neck to his shoulder were tense as cable.

"You look . . . wet," she said, hugging the towel to her. "I'm sorry."

"It's too late for sorry, McCleod." He shook his head slowly. "I want satisfaction. I want you rolling in that surf the way I was a few minutes ago. I want to hear you howl."

"Ah, come on," she said, backing to the dresser, "that's so adolescent. Couldn't we just—"

"Put on a suit," he said, "or I'll do it for you."

The panties slipped from her hand and dropped to the floor. "*Marc—*"

"That's what they call me," he said, crossing the room. He caught hold of her towel by its upper edge and gave it a yank, drawing her toward him.

"Stop it," she said, yanking back.

"Stop me," he challenged.

Sasha checked the retort on her tongue. He looked as if he might not be kidding, and she couldn't risk antagonizing him any more than she already had.

He tugged on the towel again, balling the material up in his fist until his hand was perilously close to her breasts.

"Marc," she said breathlessly, her heart racing, "stop this. I said I was sorry."

"No, you're not. You loved it. I could hear you squealing with delight."

He was close, so close that Sasha could feel the quickening force of his breath. She even caught the salty, musky scent of his skin as his hand flexed on the towel. "What are you going to do?" she asked as his fingers grazed her bare skin, thrilling her, burning her.

"I'm not quite sure," he said. "I had one thing in mind when I came in, but somehow drowning you doesn't have the same appeal now." He stared into her eyes. "What would you like me to do?"

"I'd like you to let go of this towel and leave."

"Are you sure?" Easing his hold on the wad of terry cloth, he slowly and very deliberately slipped his fingers over the knot that was holding the towel in place at her breasts.

She shuddered as his knuckles pressed against the flushed warmth of her skin. Her nipples contracted so abruptly, so painfully, it brought a gasp to her lips. "This . . . isn't fair," she whispered, glancing down at his hand. The sight of his fingers nestled in the soft cleft between her breasts sent a bolt of lightning through her body.

"Fair?" He laughed softly, huskily. "A woman who trips her opponent in a race sure as hell doesn't play by the rules, does she?"

"That was just for fun."

"So is this." He brushed a jeweled bead of water from her collarbone with his thumb and pulled her closer, nearly undoing the towel. "You are so damn beautiful, McCleod."

His hand curled into her cleavage and Sasha could feel her heartbeat slamming against his fingers. The exquisite sensations in her breasts drew her gaze to the bronzed strength of his coiled fingers, the rugged bones of his wrist, and the corded muscles of his forearm.

"And so damn willful—"

His voice was raspy and soft, but its underlying note of steel told her he was a man who didn't stop until he got what he wanted. And he wanted her. The satisfaction he was after now wouldn't come from tossing her into the surf. It was about taking her into his arms, into his bed. She could feel herself trembling beneath his fingers.

Marc was aware of her tremors too. They fed a current of excitement to his groin. The perfumed scent of her skin was an aphrodisiac.

"I don't approve of this, Renaud—not one bit."

Lord, that voice, he thought. It was delicious. She had the quivering huskiness in her voice of a woman who wanted to taste the forbidden fruit, to do all the things with a man she knew she shouldn't.

"You don't approve? Of what? This?" He drew his forefinger along the golden rise of one lush breast and watched her flinch. "My touching you? Is that why your heart's so wild?"

The rich amber of her eyes deepened with sensuality. A raspy warning was all she could manage. "I could scream for Arturo."

"Yes, you could . . . but you won't. You don't want to wake up from this dream anymore than I do."

She averted her beautiful eyes as a sexual flush crept up her breasts, radiating out from where he touched her with his forefinger. Her tiny whimper sounded like surrender, and Marc's response was instantaneous. Damn, he swore silently, it was too swift, too hot. Too hard. His gut muscles strained against the urgency, against the fire that infused his veins and surged into his loins.

"Somebody had better scream," he said, his laughter abrupt and harsh, "before I do something crazy." He released her with a half-breathed curse and tugged her towel back into place.

Sasha made no attempt to hide her astonishment. One puny remark about calling for Arturo had stopped him? "That's it?" she asked, feeling her skin burn and tingle where his hands had been. "You're giving up that easily?"

A smile shadowed his features. "Giving up? That's an interesting way to put it."

"I meant only that you seem rather relentless. I didn't expect you to behave like, well—"

He shrugged. "Like a gentleman? Don't overestimate me. Maybe I stopped because a frontal assault wasn't the best way to get what I wanted."

"And what is . . . the best way?"

"A sneak attack." His eyes flashed a warning signal, but Sasha's reflexes weren't nearly quick enough. She caught at the towel as he grabbed the edge and flicked it right out of her hands and off her body.

Sasha's gasp hit the air like a balloon exploding.

Nothing could have prepared Marc for the sight of her naked body . . . the creamy white bikini lines, the firm, golden flesh. Her breasts were high and full with dusky-pink aureoles and a translucence that accentuated their swollen state. He could even see a faint blue tracing of veins. Her legs were miles long, and yet, despite her obvious muscle tone, they had a delicate, shivery quality that made his chest ache.

He knew what was supposed to happen next, at least his body did, but his mind was fighting to comprehend the beauty, the grace expressed in every inch of her proud, trembling pose. His intuition was telling him what the spike of arousal in his groin couldn't, that loving her was going to be a mind-blowing, metaphysical experience.

Sasha was paralyzed, a riot of emotion locked in her throat. Her experience with men wasn't vast, but she had never seen a man look at her the way Marc Renaud was looking at her now, with such raw desire in his eyes. A part of her questioned why she didn't cover herself, why she stood there, breathless with shock, naked and flushed in his gaze.

"Lord," Marc said, walking to her. The rigid muscles of his arm ached as he framed her throat with his hand and pulled her to him.

Behind him, the ocean thundered relentlessly against massive cliffs, and a coastal gust sent the patio door flying open. His body shuddered, registering the sounds, but in his mind he barely heard them.

Sasha didn't hear them either.

A moan came out of her as she let herself be drawn into his arms, a moan that was full of awe at her own helplessness. *A river,* she thought, *there is a raging river of feeling inside me, dragging me under.* She was weak with the sensations that were streaming through her body. Whatever strength she might have had to resist him was lost as she felt the first contact of his thighs against hers. The sensation of his damp jeans, icy cool against her hipbones, brought a gasp to her lips.

He tilted her head up and stared down at her, warming her with the shimmering blue heat of his eyes. "What the hell *are* you doing to me?" he whispered. "I don't even know my own name."

It was the same question he'd asked during their rehearsal, and this time, as before, there was a jaggedness to it. She knew pain was fueling him, and she wanted to ask why—and what it had to do with her, but the words never made it past her lips. She lost touch with everything but her own frantic heartbeat as his hand rode up her spine, drawing her closer until her breasts brushed his chest and her nipples peaked against the erotic dusting of dark hair there.

He fit himself to her body, his hips testing hers, grinding rhythmically as he lifted her hair and murmured sensual things into the hollow of her neck. He told her how lush and sexy her breasts were against his ribs, how sweet her skin tasted on his lips, sweet and utterly feminine. Excitement raced through her veins as his arousal burned its dimensions into her flesh, hot and hard in the valley created by her hipbones.

It came to Sasha then, in a split second of reality, that she was stark naked in the arms of the director of the picture she'd been hired for, that she was teetering on the brink of an abandoned encounter with Marc Renaud, the man she'd clashed with almost continually until this point. A torrid scenario of seduction and ravishment engulfed her imagination.

She pressed a hand to his chest in a crazy attempt to stop the runaway train they were on. Sensing her resistance, he stroked her face and thrilled her with his mouth, brushing his lips along the length of hers, back and forth.

The awareness that swept through Sasha was

languid and muted, a voice calling from a distance. *Am I supposed to let him kiss me this way? Am I supposed to let him do these things?*

The answer that came zinging back was no.

But did she want him to? As his mouth pressed into hers and he stroked the delicate tip of her tongue with his, a response snuck through the call of her conscience. *Yes . . . ohhh, yes.*

Releasing the breath she'd been holding, she curled her arms around his waist. She'd never been so aware of the male form before, of coiled muscularity and jutting strength. She thrilled to the contours of his thighs, the washboard ridges of his belly.

Marc closed his eyes and sighed as Sasha's fingertips did a butterfly's caress along the waistband of his jeans. He sensed her acquiescence, and it beat in his blood—but he wanted more. He wanted surrender, on his terms. He'd held back from touching her too intimately—and that was no easy task with her naked body pressed against him. The silky shiver of her breasts when she moved was agonizing. Every nerve, every muscle in his body anticipated what would happen when he eased his hands up her rib cage, cupped her breasts and kissed their delicate flesh, arousing the nipples to dusky pink buds. Yes, he wanted to touch her, to taste and arouse her, all of her. But he also wanted to hear her purr, to feel her shudder and arch against him like a cat. He wanted to hear that wild animal cry of need.

Her skin was satin-cool as he slid his palms down the curves of her midriff to the high, flared bones of her hips. She trembled under his caress and looked up at him, her eyes wide and wary. The sparks in her amber irises were iridescent, like stars at twilight. Desire shot through him as he imagined those sparks igniting into flame.

"Have you ever been touched here?" he asked, tucking her hair behind the graceful curve of her ear. "Like this?" Stroking the petals of her lobe with his forefinger, he delved inside with the intimacy of a lover. Her lips parted expectantly, and her fingers dug into the muscles of his back. Yes, just like that, he thought. *Respond to me, Sasha. Let me know you want this. Show me how much.* He could feel the need, the ripening passion in her, but he was waiting for the sighs, the little cries, the signs of surrender. This was not a woman to be hurried into bed. She was the type to be aroused for hours and hours, days if need be, before finally spreading open her sleek legs and taking that heartbreaking trip to paradise.

Holding himself in check, he brushed his thumb over her parted lips and shuddered at their softness. A fantasy flashed in his mind . . . of her mouth, sweet and hot as she moved her lips over his, and then erotically light as she trailed kisses down his neck and his chest to the rigid planes of his stomach. A stab of pain pierced his consciousness. He could feel the urgency in his own body, the hard ache between his legs. No woman had ever stirred his imagination the way she did. He fought down the urge to hook his hands beneath her knees, lift her and curl her legs around his waist, fought the urge to drive himself into her deeply, mindlessly, thrusting until he was lost forever in the hurtling bliss of bodies and heartbeats.

Behind him, the patio door was swaying open and shut, hurling shadows across the room. The ocean roared like a lonely, angry lion.

Surrendering a notch to the hunger inside him, Marc pressed his hardness into her belly and insinuated his tongue into her warm, soft mouth, tasting deeply, stealing her sweetness. Her flushed skin was a slipstream of sensuality running up and down the length of him. Her breasts were vibrantly pillowed against his ribs. Easing back a little, he touched her lower lip with his tongue, moistening its silken pleats—and groaning with pleasure as she opened her mouth to him. The invitation was wanton and inflaming. It was irresistible. He thrust into her again and again.

The whimper that trembled through her was anguished and sweet. It aroused and enraged every male instinct Marc had. She was the roaring thunder in his head, the chain lightning in his groin. He had to have her. *Now.*

Breaking the kiss, he turned with her still in his arms and stooped to pick her up. She seemed almost fragile and much too light for her height as he lifted her into his arms.

She tossed her hair from her eyes, and he was struck by the dreamy, dizzy shyness in her smile. She looked awed and apprehensive and outrageously sexy all at once. Suddenly, snuggling into him, she buried her face in the crook of his shoulder and emitted a sound that made his heart catch.

"Sasha?"

She looked up at him at last. He searched her whiskey eyes and, without thinking, bent to kiss her.

"Marc—" Her breath rushed against his lips. Gently she pressed her fingers to his mouth and held him back.

It was the unsteadiness in her voice that stopped him. "What is it?" he asked.

"I'm afraid—"

"Afraid of making love?"

"No . . ." She looked up at him, her shoulders lifting with a deep breath. "Of *falling* in love."

The jolt of surprise inside Marc was so painful he could hardly breathe. He'd never seen her so open, so vulnerable. But wasn't that exactly what he'd wanted? Vulnerability? Surrender? His heart pounded in his chest. At last he set her down and caught her by the arms, hesitating, gazing at her, and finally holding her away from him. Her hair flowed like corn silk around her body, and her mouth, unsteady and still slightly swollen from their kiss, bewitched him. Falling in love? With him? Was that what she was saying?

The door swung open behind them, and this time Marc heard it all, the deep roar of the ocean, the creaking and groaning of wood and glass against the hinges. The sounds resonated through his consciousness like a storm warning, but he didn't respond. In that moment of staring into Sasha's rich, wild-honey eyes, he could taste the sweetness, the hot, stinging need in his throat. His entire body hardened at the thought of making love to her. But his mind, his mind was reeling from what she'd said. His restricted breathing did what the elements couldn't do. It warned him of the pain, the heartbreak he would be letting them both in for.

In that split second of accountability, he knew nothing but grief could come out of an encounter with her. He couldn't make love to her. He couldn't let himself love her—or her him. Marc Renaud destroyed the people who loved him. Marc Renaud left emotional wreckage and dead bodies behind him. . . .

"Marc—"

Her voice brought him back. He was holding her. His hands were locked on her arms, and her skin was whitened, bloodless under the grip of his fingers. He released her abruptly and backed away, crouching to pick up the towel.

"Marc? What is it?"

The ocean pounded in his ears, its noise deafening. A moment later he was in the alcove, closing the swinging French doors, and her unexpected touch on his shoulder made him flinch and jerk around.

She veered back, frightened. "What's wrong?"

He knew it must be the wildness in his eyes. She couldn't hear the horror, the echoes in his head, and there was nothing he could tell her, nothing she would ever understand—or be able to forgive. "You don't want to fall in love with me, Sasha." His throat constricted, producing a huskiness in his voice. "You don't want to make that mistake."

"Is that what this is all about?" she whispered. "Because I said I was afraid of falling in love?"

He cut her off quickly, slicing through her confusion, through his own emotion, with words that were cold and heartless, words that gave away nothing. "This was a mistake, Sasha, a monumental miscalculation. You and I, here, in this house? I must have been crazy to let this happen."

"Why? Why was it a mistake?"

"Because I've got a picture to salvage. Because my credibility's at stake. I'm in deep enough trouble without adding a fling with the star's replacement to the list."

She was bewildered, distraught. He was hurting her with his lies. He was hurting himself, but he had no choice. Blocking her stricken expression from his mind, he brushed past her and walked to the door. He was good at this, shutting things out of his life, people out of his life. Yes, he was good at cutting out the offending spot. Only this time, *he* was that spot. "I'll be staying at the studio from now on," he added without turning back.

As the door closed behind him, Sasha released the startled moan in her throat. The room was damp and deeply chilled, a briny musk permeating the air. Covered in goose flesh, she wrapped the huge towel around her and sat on the bed. Her body trembled with shock and disbelief. Her emotional world was in pieces, debris scattered to the winds. And she was cold, so cold she might never be warm again.

It seemed like hours later that finally, in the lengthening shadow of her silence, a protective numbness began to seep through her limbs, into her thoughts. The lethargy soothed her, dulled her senses, but it couldn't block out one ringing certainty. She knew it as surely as she knew the beat of her own heart. Marc Renaud's conflict, the brilliant white-hot rage at the core of his being, had nothing to do with his movie.

Eight

The following day the weather broke and the location shooting began in an isolated inlet south of Newport Beach. Under a crayon-blue sky, the crew prepared for that day's sequence of action shots, hauling lights and sound equipment onto the loamy sand while the mobile generator units hummed in the background. Sasha milled around in her bathing suit and coverup, drinking decaffeinated tea and waiting for someone to signal her that they were ready to go. She seemed to be the only one with nothing to do.

Marc was huddled with his cinematographer, discussing possible shots, and Carlos, her costar, stood down at the water's edge, staring out in deep concentration. Finding his center, Sasha supposed. She would like to have gone down and talked with Carlos—she would like to have talked with *anyone* at the moment to ease her sense of isolation, even the caterer dispensing coffee and danish—but she knew better than to impede the frantic pace of the activity around her.

They were scheduled for pickup shots that day,

of Lisa swimming and body-surfing. The script called for an energetic, high-spirited Lisa, the woman she was *before* Jesse intervened in her life and fouled up the works. Not unlike my situation, Sasha thought, wistful as she considered Marc. `

She watched her director walk toward the water's edge and hesitate, scoping out shots with his cinematographer in tow. He scanned the horizon, contemplated an outcropping of jagged black rocks down the beach, and turned to consider the cliffs behind them. He might have been a Native American in his Navajo serape and jeans—until you got a look at those powder-blue eyes. In truth, he was all she could think about, all she had thought about since the previous night. Like Lisa's, her life seemed to have been altered, too, by the unexpected intercession of a complex man.

A tiny, perfect seashell was nestled in the sand near Sasha's feet. She turned it over with her bare toe, saw the crack in its delicately ridged surface—and a thought ricocheted through her consciousness. *Lisa's life, her untroubled existence, had been destroyed because of Jesse.*

Foreboding prickled Sasha's skin, chilling her. She rubbed her arms, her thoughts veering back to Marc and the way he'd surprised her when she'd arrived an hour earlier. She'd expected icy control, a frost-breathing dragon. Instead, he'd seemed subdued when he'd greeted her. His eyes were shadowed and red-rimmed, as though he'd slept badly or drunk too much. She couldn't deny the coldness in him, but as always there was something else just below the surface that tugged at her emotions. The occasional glimpses she stole when he didn't know she was looking revealed a man who was angry at life, a man psychologically bruised and bloodied by the mere fact of his existence. Yes, he was hurting, she was sure of that—and even more certain that he would never admit it. What kind of a miracle would it take to reach the man inside those self-imposed walls?

She broke away from her solitary reflections, dropped her empty paper teacup into a portable waste bin, and walked to the edge of the chaotic activity. The truth was, she was half afraid of what she might find if she penetrated Marc Renaud's glacial barriers.

"Sasha—"

She started as a hand touched her arm, and Jimmy, the production assistant, appeared at her elbow with a warm, reassuring grin.

"We're ready to go," he said, shaking a thumb at the foaming ocean. "Hope the water's not too cold. I suggested a heated pool and a wave machine, but our director's a purist."

Laughing, Sasha shrugged out of her coverup and handed it to him. A cool coastal breeze made her shiver as she looked up and saw Marc's gaze on her. He was off to himself by a stand of reflectors, and for several seconds he fixed her with his unwavering scrutiny, taking in the high-slashed legs of her one-piece suit, the glossy red material, and the scooped neckline that crowded her generous breasts into rounds of sun-brushed gold.

Warmth crept up Sasha's throat, washing her in a flood tide of self-awareness. For a man who considered her a distraction, he certainly was indulging himself. Every silent brush of his eyes on her person reminded her that he had touched her there, kissed her there, pressed his body against her there. A soft thrill rolled through her like the foamy waves lapping up onshore. Before she could stop it, a slide show of yesterday's encounter flashed through her mind . . . her naked body, wet from the shower, his, still damp from the ocean . . . the steamy scent of straining flesh, the hot, sweet sighs and soul-deep need.

She brought an arm to her waist, hugging herself protectively. It was an unconscious gesture, and one she would never have made if she'd realized how vulnerable and desirable it made her appear.

In the pleasure centers of Marc Renaud's brain, the gesture registered as though he himself were hugging her. His skin tingled, and his senses came alive to the imagined silkiness of her suit, made warm with her body heat. Breathing in, he filled the hollow space in his chest. "I'm ready if you are," he said.

She studied the water. "What am I supposed to do?"

"Run like a kid who's just been let out of school, splash through the waves, dive in. Be joyous, feel the freedom."

A moment later the camera was rolling and Sasha was racing toward the surf. Marc watched her, struck by the smooth flow of her limbs, the willowy strength in her slender frame. He trusted his cameraman to catch the sun splashing off her white-gold hair and the halo effect of the horizon as it silhouetted her movements. Pressure built in his stomach as he thought about how her long, finely muscled body had felt under his hands. Just for a moment he allowed himself the luxury of imagining her beneath him, on top of him, rolling in a tangled, sensual heap as he moved deeply inside her body.

The stab of longing he felt was closer to pain than pleasure. She was infecting his thoughts, invading his senses like a rampant, self-perpetuating virus. All night he'd dreamed and thrashed and bolted out of his sleep with her name on his lips. It was hell, what his mind was doing to him, sweet, searing hell.

He'd planned to stop by the beach house that night and pick up some clothes. No way, he'd decided. If he went near the place, he would never be able to keep his hands off her. Watching her dive into the surf and bob up, sleek and wet as a golden seal, he reminded himself again that a career—*his* career—and a multimillion-dollar movie were at stake. It was reason enough to keep his distance from her.

His body responded with a mutinous flash of desire, and he made himself a promise. If they were ever together again, he vowed silently—someday, somewhere, after all this was over—he was going to make every damn one of his fantasies come true.

The remainder of the week went quickly for Sasha, almost too quickly. With Marc away from the house, time slipped by like the proverbial sand sifting through curled fingers. The chance to be with him was getting more remote with each day that passed. Sasha didn't give much thought to what she would do if she ever got that chance. Something powerful was driving her, some energy that was distinct from any other need she'd ever known. She didn't know how, when, or even why, but a vague sense of desperation had taken hold of her.

She saw him every day on location, but the action sequences were going so smoothly, they rarely spoke beyond his stage directions. As the week drew on, she spent her days increasingly aware of his darkening moods—and her nights standing on her terrace foolishly wondering if she should try to make contact with him before it was all over. Despite his brooding posture, she'd seen the look in his eyes many times, even during filming.

The *look*. It was the concentrated, half-lidded stare of a man who had dark and passionate things on his mind. Any woman who messed with that look was asking for trouble. Sasha knew it as surely as she knew daffodils bloomed in the spring—and yet she couldn't subdue the urge to see him again, to be alone with him.

A week later they wrapped up the location shooting, and Sasha returned to the beach house thoroughly depressed. She'd received rave reviews on her work from everyone, including Marc, which might have thrilled her except for the fact that her stint in the movie was now virtually over.

She spent the entire evening in a tug-of-war with herself, staring at the phone as she contemplated the prospect of calling him at the studio. She must have picked up the receiver and clanked it back down a dozen times. No, dammit, she told herself on the thirteenth clank, *he* walked out. If one of them was going to capitulate, it would have to be him.

Much later that night, sleepless and searching out a midnight snack in the kitchen, Sasha heard the service door to the garage area quietly open and close. "Bink?" she called out, tugging the lapels of her white satin nightshirt together as she peered down the dark hallway.

"Bink doesn't seem to be around."

Marc's voice came from behind her. She whirled and saw him standing in the open terrace doors that led to the deck. His arm was propped on the doorjamb above his head, and he was leaning into it. Despite his casualness, he looked world-weary and vaguely predatory with a heavy five o'clock shadow along the planes of his jaw. Lord, those eyes of his were cold, she thought, her stomach dipping. They were snow crystals shimmering against a blue sky. "To what do I owe the honor?" she asked.

"This isn't a social call." His gaze brushed over her, absently noting the length of sleek thigh exposed by the side slash of her shirt. "Unless you call picking up some clean underwear a social call."

"Depends on how hard up you are," Sasha mumbled, not intending him to hear it.

He did, unfortunately. "Things have been worse" —his eyes drifted to the shimmer of her breasts under their satin covering—"but not much."

Sasha waved a hand toward the refrigerator. "I was just going to have a snack," she said.

"How about a fifth of something, preferably one hundred proof." He swung open the refrigerator door, investigated its contents, and pulled out a bottle of red wine. "I guess this will have to do." He worked out the cork, offered her the bottle. "Join me?"

Thoroughly disenchanted with his cavalier attitude, she wrinkled her nose. Dropping by to pick up some clean underwear, indeed. This was hardly the capitulation she had in mind. "I'll leave you to your bottle then," she said pointedly, "and your Jockey shorts."

She took a step back, swung around, and started for the hallway, expecting him to say something, praying he'd say something. She took two steps, three, made a slight pause as she reached the threshold of the door.

"Sasha—"

Her breath locked in her chest. That wasn't the voice of an indifferent man. Oh, no, that was the voice of a man about to go against his better judgment, a man succumbing to his own dark instincts. There was need, self-directed anger, and raw sexual energy in the way he said her name. She waited, her hand still clutching the lapel of her shirt, waited there in suspended animation. She didn't know for how long. . . .

"*Sasha*," he whispered from behind. A moment later she felt his fingers at the nape of her neck, lifting her hair. Automatically she tilted her head to welcome the sweet, cool touch on her skin. His mouth, she realized, his soft, heartbreaking mouth.

His hands closed on her arms in a hard, possessive grip that thrilled her. Sasha's senses sharpened painfully. She could hear his breathing, feel its warmth. The smooth hum of the refrigerator droned in the background, and somewhere beyond that waves crashed onto the beach. He swung her around, stared down at her with eyes that ripped right through her heart, eyes that said *I'm dying without you.*

Pain filled her throat. Sweet and stinging hot, it brought tears to her eyes. "Marc?" she whispered, reaching up to touch him. "Oh, Lord, Marc. What's wrong?"

He avoided the caress of her hand and pulled her closer, his breath laced with low, whispering torment.

"You . . . you're what's wrong. You're like a dull knife blade cutting through my body, opening me up and leaving me to bleed. You remind me of everything I was, dammit. Worse, you make me want it again, all of it, all those things I can't have."

"What? What can't you have?"

His hands flexed on her arms. "That white-hot fire inside you," he said softly, searching her face for the answers, "the purity, the uncompromising passion. Lord." He laughed bitterly. "You still believe in right and wrong. You still believe in people—" His mouth twisted, and his eyes glittered brilliantly, sheened with anger and unrepentant tears.

Sasha's heart wrenched. Her confusion mounted. "I don't understand. . . ."

He drew in a deep breath and released it. Bowing his head, he was suddenly, immutably, closed to her, to life. "Yeah—" he said on an exhaled breath. "Well, why should you understand? Why should anyone? Hell, I'm probably ranting about nothing anyway. I have a tendency to do that."

He let go of her arms and walked away. He dug a hand into his shirt pocket, pulled out a cigarette from a pack of Gauloises, and lit it. "Look, I'm sorry. It was asinine of me to run off at the mouth that way." He turned back to her, smoke streaming from his nostrils. His eyes were dull and dry. "Let's just forget it happened."

"No, Marc—"

But he'd already shaken off the whole episode. He picked up the wine bottle and held it high before taking a long drink. "Things to do," he said.

Distraught, Sasha watched him stride from the room. "What are you running from?" she cried.

He hesitated briefly in the darkness of the hallway. "That's easy . . . myself."

She heard him climbing the stairs, and a hot flush of anger impelled her. "That doesn't make you any less of a coward, Marc-André Renaud!"

A door cracked shut on the second story.

Sasha brought her fist down on the countertop in sheer frustration. He was escaping to his inner sanctum, of course. She stormed to the hall closet, dragged out a huge overcoat that probably belonged to him, and pulled it on. Why did she care anyway? He obviously didn't want her help. He was probably beyond help! Why did she give a damn what was bugging that lost cause of a Frenchman? *And why was she aching in every cell of her body to be with him?*

The breeze off the ocean cooled her flushed face as she stood on the terrace, hugging her arms and feeling very much alone. A sea gull's cry cut through her, increasing her sense of isolation. She missed her home, the health club, T.C. She'd been separated too long from everyone she cared about, everything she knew and understood. It hit her all at once that she desperately wanted to get away from Malibu, from sets and movie studios, from all of it!

Moments later she was in the sprawling garage, staring at the Corvette and fighting off a crazy urge to hot-wire it again and head for Redondo Beach. Torn by confusing impulses, she stole into the interior of the car and fell back against the seat, rolling her head up, breathing in the leathery scent of tuck-and-roll upholstery, the lingering vapors of plush new carpeting.

Absently fingering the ignition, she was assessing her chances of getting to a pay telephone to call a taxi when the driver's side door of the Corvette flew open. "Oh!" Sasha bolted forward in shock as Marc crouched in the doorway of the car, his hand resting on the interior handle.

"Going somewhere?"

"You nearly scared the life out of me!" she said, each word a soft squeak. The traces of amusement in his eyes sent a bolt of fury through her heart. If her reaction was fueled more by pent-up

frustration than by fear, it propelled her nonethe-
less. "That's it!" she vowed. "That's it. I'm getting
out of this asylum. Yes, I am going somewhere!"
She jerked and fought with the huge overcoat as
she struggled to get out of the car. "I'm going
home, Marc—and I don't give a damn whether
you like it or not!"

She shoved past him, breaking through the barrier of his arms in her passionate determination
to get out of the garage, and out of his life. If this
was the man's idea of a good time, she didn't
want any part of it.

She nearly made good her bid for freedom. Striding across the garage, she was just a yard or so
from the door when he grabbed a fistful of the
overcoat's voluminous material and brought her
to a skidding halt.

"Correct me if I'm wrong," he said, catching
hold of the coat's lapel and spinning her around,
"but are you angry?"

"What gave you the first clue?" Angry? *Angry?*
It was all she could do not to haul off and slug
him.

"Sasha—"

"Don't call me that!"

He blinked, momentarily charming in his baf-
flement. "What would you like me to call you? It's
your name."

"I know, but I hate the way you say it." No,
that's not quite true, the quickening pace of her
heart reminded her. *You love the way he says it.
You wish he'd never stop saying it.* She took a
breath, appalled at her own weakening resolve. "I
suppose you think it's funny, sneaking up on
unsuspecting women? Scaring them half to death?"

"No, I don't."

"Yes you do. You *smiled.*"

He shrugged, and smiled again. "I didn't think it was any funnier than you did when you tripped me."

"Oh, so this is payback? Good, then we're even." She pulled free of his hold and started for the open door, moaning as he snagged her wrist and swung her back around. "Will you stop manhandling me!"

"Will you stop running away?"

Before Sasha could protest, he had her backed up against the garage wall.

"Why can't you and I ever seem to have a conversation like normal people do?" he asked softly. "Whatever the reason, I've got a couple of things to settle with you."

Her heart leapt into her throat. "What things?"

"First of all, this isn't payback." His eyes flashed a drenching, dizzying blue. "And second, *nobody* calls me a coward, Sasha, not even you."

Even if she could have fought off the enchantment of his eyes, his voice would have snared her in its visceral web. It was suffused with the hard poignancy of need and desire. It was a burning love song. The heat of his hands penetrated the overcoat, and the scent of liquor was potent on his breath. Those signals tugged at her, warned her. He didn't seem to be inebriated, but that didn't mean he wasn't dangerously uninhibited. "I didn't mean coward in the physical sense," she tried to explain.

"What sense, then?"

Aware of the concrete's chill against her shoulders, she summoned her wits. Every rational cell in her brain was telling her to be careful how she handled the question, and him. "Well, think about it," she said, her voice soft, requesting reason. "I mean, what is a coward really, but a man who employs caution, a man who looks before he leaps—"

He shook his head slowly. "Sorry, won't wash. I do my best leaping blindfolded. Now, why don't you tell me the truth? Or maybe you're employing a little caution yourself?"

Sasha didn't pretend to be a skilled liar. She wasn't even much good at the little white kind, and yet to be so easily exposed was embarrassing. "All right, then," she said, provoked as much by his wry expression as by the pride she took in her own honesty. "You want the truth? The unvarnished truth? You *are* a coward, Marc. You're terrified of getting involved with a woman like me, a real woman."

He blinked in slow, droll amazement and mouthed her last three words as though he couldn't believe he'd heard them. The glitter in his eyes was devastating as he stared down at her, holding her transfixed for so long that Sasha thought the earth must have stopped in its orbit. Everything seemed to be in a state of suspended animation, including her heart.

"I must admit," he said, running his hands down her arms to her wrists, "you've got me curious now." He tugged her closer, bent to her mouth in breathless hesitation, and then nipped the curve of her uptilted chin instead. Murmuring a shocking proposition under his breath, he pressed a stingingly sweet kiss to her lips. "How am I doing for a guy who's terrified?"

Sasha felt as though she'd been sideswiped by an orbiting comet. "You're doing fine," she said, her disorientation skewing the words a little, "but that kiss was a sh—shade too sexual in nature, and therefore . . ."

Her voice evaporated as she perceived his thumbnail skimming circles in her palm, drifting, dipping. It was as intimate, as sexual an overture as she'd ever experienced in her life.

"Therefore what?"

Staring into his eyes, she sank slowly into a fathomless pool of silver water. Her breath spun out lacework in her head. She was lost in that infinite moment between heartbeats, where senses recede and become sensation. She was submerged, weightless, floating in warmth. From somewhere a muted voice came to her, soft and dreamy—her own voice—and she was saying something perfectly rational. "Therefore, I'm betting that it's *emotional* involvement you're afraid of, Marc Renaud, not sexual."

"No, you're wrong—" His breath traced her skin like an erotic fingerstroke. "It is sex, Sasha. With you. *Anything with you.* Sex, love, all of it."

She could hear the need in him, the fierce poignancy, and behind it a voice was whispering to her, low and beautiful . . . *if you go, if you leave me now, I'll die.* . . .

It was Jesse's voice, Marc's voice. Filled with longing, it pulled at her emotions. "Let me be what you need." The words were drawn out of her with a whispering torment she couldn't control. "Please, I can be what you need."

His jaw clenched against something dark and powerful inside him. "What I need may frighten you, Sasha. It sure as hell frightens me."

"I'm not frightened." But she was.

She reached up to stroke his mouth, her fingers trembling. His eyes darkened with dizzying speed.

Sasha was swimming in weakness, in sensation as he steadied her with one hand while he stripped the overcoat off her.

The coat settled around her ankles, its soft folds imprisoning her. *I can be what you need*, she cried silently as he pressed her to the wall again, his hands strong and possessive, searingly hot against her skin. Her satin nightshirt fluttered against her body, and her nipples budded in response. A soft aching welled thickly in her loins. Of its own will her body was preparing her for the rich, drugging pleasure of his touch, his mouth, his body. She closed her eyes and let her head drop back.

Everything spun away from her but his hands. They touched her everywhere but those tender places she ached for him, her breasts, her womanhood. With tactile grace he drove her to a pitch of near frenzy, caressing her through the sliding silk fabric of her shirt. As he stroked her thighs, she could feel the fathomless pool, deep inside her now, rippling. It was torment. She'd never felt such beauty, such yearning.

His fingers trembled on her skin. "Want me," he said, shocking her as he insinuated his knee between her legs and eased them apart. "Want me, Sasha, more than you want your next breath of air."

She moaned as he pressed up against the most vibrant part of her body. He was transfusing her veins with fire, melting her limbs with a dreamy gush of erotic languor. "I do" was all she could whisper. "Lord, I do."

Her words hung in the air, shimmering, gathering energy, exploding in Marc's brain. He hardened instantly, everywhere. Sweet Lord he thought, this was what he needed—all he would ever need—this beautiful, abandoned woman. She was the cure. As she moved against his leg, excitement shot through him, pooling hotly in his loins. His fingers tightened on her arms.

His nerves were so exquisitely attuned to her, he could feel the shuddering sigh that passed through her body. He could read the message in her eyes as they drifted open briefly and met his. Full of dazed wonder and urgency, her whiskey gaze said one thing to him and one thing only. She was his. He could do what he wanted with her.

His body's reaction was instantaneous. His legs weakened, and his stomach muscles spasmed, locking off desire. With slow, torturous control, he worked open the buttons of her nightshirt and drew the silky material off her shoulder, exposing one delicately veined, translucent breast.

For a moment all he could do was stare at her. She looked too fragile to touch, as though the slightest pressure of his fingers would leave marks on her skin. She was a creamy rose petal, her perfection easily bruised. And yet the banked fire in her amber eyes was wanton and sensual. She wanted to be touched. She wanted to be handled. She was drugged, intoxicated with wanting.

"Marc," she whispered, her shoulders rising, her flesh quivering, "please . . . put your hands on me."

Lightning flashed straight through to the core of him. Drawing the shirt off her other shoulder, he bared her to the waist and choked back a savage sound at the sight of her. She arched forward, moaning, and her breasts filled his hands. Her weight, her silky warmth, made his arms ache with sensations—wild little bursts of energy that blazed through his muscles and battered his senses with agonizing pleasure.

Blond hair flew as she tossed her head and let

herself fall against him. A whimper of desire caught in her throat and she cupped her fingers over his, pressing him into her flesh. The fire in her eyes was a plea, a passionate challenge. *Now, now!* it blazed. *Don't make me wait any longer.*

He dragged her back to him, and she went a little crazy in his arms, moaning, sighing, tangling her hands in his hair. He closed his eyes, his belly filling with fire. He'd never known a woman who triggered such powerful, gut-wrenching needs. Cupping her buttocks, he brought her into the fit of his thighs and thrust himself against her softness. He took her lips at the same time, and her response was a throaty cry that raged in his blood. He relinquished her mouth and bent to her breasts, sipping, sucking, unable to get close enough to her.

A moment later he was aware of nothing but his thundering heartbeat and the pounding heat between his legs. He crushed her nightshirt in his fists and drew it up her thighs, riveted by the cries in her throat, the shimmering softness of her legs. She was naked underneath the shirt, naked and tender as a baby.

With one frantic tug Marc released the button and zipper on his jeans. He hooked a hand beneath each of her knees, lifted her to his waist, and curled her legs around him. She straddled him gracefully, entwining her arms around his neck and gasping in surprise as he pressed against the golden triangle of her sex. Astonished at his own control, he entered her gradually, probing, seducing away the natural resistance of her muscles with rhythmic half strokes.

He took it slowly, easily, caressing her with the aching hardness between his legs, priming her until she was crying and bucking and breathing out his name. Curled around his body, she was a trembling, unrestrained lover. *"Yes, like this,"* she whispered, lacing her fingers into the thickness of his hair, arching up and lowering herself onto him. *"I need you like this."*

Out of his mind with desire, Marc pressed her tender, undulating body to the wall and drove into her again and again. He was oblivious to everything but the primitive, pounding urges of his body—and his desperate need for her. She was the hot, sweet pressure in his loins, the cinch closing around his heart, the eternal wonder in his soul.

They rocked and kissed and clung to each other. In the final moments of completion, Sasha felt his power streaming inside her and her body tightened to bursting. In her mind she saw the golden spiral of an exploding star. It was glorious, the most acute pleasure she'd ever known. In the last brilliant seconds before the blaze engulfed her, she called out a name, his.

Nine

In the first flushed moments of recovery, Marc wrapped Sasha in the overcoat and pulled her into his arms. Swaying with tenderness, he held her head against the curve of his neck and gentled her with whispers. When her tremors subsided, he shifted back to look at her.

"Are you all right?" he asked, molding a hand to her face protectively. Aware of the staccato beat of her pulse beneath his fingers, he drew an arc in the downy blond hair wisps at her temple.

She nodded and pressed herself to him again as though for warmth and some kind of reassurance. Marc's heart moved oddly in his chest. He enfolded her tightly, his hand squeezing into a fist at her nape. It was a strange, sweet moment of bonding, and he found himself wishing it would never end.

The soft thunder of the ocean drifted to them through the doorway, ushered in by a breeze that was increasingly chilly and damp with condensation. As the mist penetrated his clothing, Marc snuggled the coat around her, savoring her delicate warmth and her small shuddering sighs.

He hadn't expected this, not from her. He'd glimpsed her vulnerability on several occasions, but nobody could have made him believe that the beautiful spitfire he'd met a week ago would respond to him with the naked abandon of this woman in his arms.

He kissed the spun silver crown of her head, and she arched her neck to look up at him. Her soft smile and the sparkle in her eyes seemed to whisper *wow*. No guilt, no regrets, no frills, just *wow*.

My sentiments exactly, he thought.

Her face was flushed and slightly abraded from his beard-rough jaw. Her hair was wild. Another man might have called her a temptress, but Marc saw her as he wanted to see her, as he needed to see her. She was pristine, with a clarity about her eyes, a purity in her passion. This woman's soul is new and clean, he thought, taking her by the hand.

A melancholy came over him as they returned to the house, and their reverential state of silence came to an end. She dropped the overcoat on a chair and turned to him, a finger pressed to her lips as though she weren't quite sure what was supposed to happen next. Finally, lifting a shoulder, she said, "I could fix us something, some coffee?"

He caught hold of her hands, his mood philosophical. "Tell me, Sasha," he asked, "are you . . . what's the word? Incorruptible?"

She gave it a moment. "Yes, I think so."

He stared into her eyes, and the melancholy inside him compressed into a tiny hot kernel of regret. For her sake he almost wished it were true. She was proud and unassailable. She was beautiful. *But she was wrong.* How do I tell her, he thought. How do I warn her that even she can be seduced? Will she believe that everyone has his fall from grace . . . his despoiler? Will she believe that with her it's me. He brought her to him, halting as their hips touched. *I'm the one who can corrupt her.*

She met his gaze, and he saw her momentary bewilderment, the sparkle of apprehension. It was as though she'd read his thoughts. And then gradually, like the morning sun creeping over a hill and refusing to believe there was anything beyond the warmth of its rays, she gazed up at him with such burning sweetness he could hardly breathe.

"Yes, I suppose I am incorruptible," she said, rifling her fingers through his hair, "unless *you* had something in mind. I might like a bad-tempered French film director to ruin me. Or to try."

She kissed him on the nose, nuzzled up his neck, and left a sharp kitten's nip on his earlobe. "Now you're marked," she murmured, rolling her eyes, realizing what she'd said. "Pardon the pun."

Marc laughed at her, disarmed, his sadness fading. "What are you doing to me?" he asked, shaking his head as he realized how many times he'd said or thought those words. All of a sudden he had to have her in his arms, to feel her heartbeat against his ribs and breathe the same air she breathed. He swept her into an embrace so abruptly, she gasped.

"I need you again," he told her.

"If I'm incorruptible," she said, "then you're insatiable."

He kissed her deeply, rimming her lips and the fine edges of her teeth with his tongue. She opened her mouth to him automatically, whimpering as he pressed into her with a deep, rhythmic thrusting that simulated the passion to come. His stomach muscles knotted with pleasure as she tightened her lips, encasing his forays and creating a friction that set his blood on fire.

He broke away, breathing huskily. "Here? In the kitchen?" he asked, freeing the buttons on her nightshirt and curving his hands to her breasts as the silky material fell away.

She pressed her hand over his as desire rekindled, and led him out onto the glass-enclosed sun deck. Naked, wordless, she melted against him, and they dropped to the chintz daybed. Their steamy passion saturated the night and beat heavily through the room around them. Marc was aware only of her warm flesh, caressing lips, and the fiery heat of her loins. They rolled and clung and writhed, her sobbing with pleasure and him moving deeply inside her, another magnificent fantasy realized.

Sasha was driven senseless with the riotous pleasure he gave her. He made love like a man possessed. She clung to him wantonly, moaning under the sweet, hammering thrusts of his thighs, the deep penetration of his tongue. One moment he was tender and unbearably gentle, cherishing her as if she were the most precious, inviolate thing he'd ever touched. The next he was invading, plunging himself into the exquisite heart of her, taking possession, taking everything she had to give.

As the crescendo of power and passion began, Marc had the answer to his question. He knew what she was doing to him. She was burning away his past like a torch held to an old photograph. When he was with her, he could block out the memories, drive them away with every aching thrust into her pliant body. She was his liberation. As long as he could hold her, make love to her, he could ward off the devils.

Afterward, their bodies still joined, they held each other. A dream flickered on the rim of their awareness, the same crazy, wistful lovers' dream. Sasha was afraid to voice it. Marc was reluctant even to think it. Was this it, they both wondered. The missing puzzle piece in their lives, the key to completion?

In the days that followed, with shooting wrapped and the movie in post-production, Marc turned *Tell Me No Lies* over to his film editors, and he and Sasha secluded themselves in the confines of the beach house, making it their hideaway. Neither of them knew exactly when the studio might decide it was time for Sasha to return to her former life.

It was enchanted, their private world. Marc's mood seemed to have lifted permanently. He ran with Sasha on the cool sand at sunrise, and at twilight they celebrated the balmy coming of spring to the Malibu coast with champagne and laughter. The tangy scent of the sea surrounded them, murmuring lovers' secrets. No matter where they were, desire breathed. An intimate touch, a whisper, and they were caught up in the sexual undertow of their passion, dragged down by some powerful current.

Sasha was dizzied and drunk with it all, happier than she'd ever been. She entertained Marc until the wee hours of the morning with the life and times of Sasha McCleod, air force brat, fitness phenomenon. She even included the bittersweet story of Alexandria, her Gypsy mother, a confidence she'd never shared anyone else.

Marc absorbed her monologues with silent admiration, marveling at her openness. He understood her fierce independence now. What he couldn't fathom was her ability to fling herself into things, to embrace them with such fervor. Very soon it would be him, he realized. He was about to become her next cause, which meant she would want to know everything about him, every blessed detail. She would expect it.

What then, he asked himself.

The week wore on, and she surprised him by biding her time. He'd almost begun to think she wasn't going to broach the topic of his past when she casually waylaid him in the Jacuzzi. They were on the deck off his bedroom, lounging in the warm bubbles and laughing at the Sunday comics.

She touched his arm. "Tell me about France," she said simply. "I've never been there."

"That could take years."

She smiled at him, delighted. "Good, I've got years."

Marc knew there was no deterring her. He began with the France of his childhood, highlighting the pleasant memories, skirting the fissures and shadows. The postwar Burgundy region, where the family estate and vineyards were located was an idyllic setting, he told her. He'd stolen away with the peasant farmers' children whenever he could to play in the Roman ruins near Vezelay, a crumbling medieval town where his passion for fantasy and filmmaking was born.

Sasha made a rapt audience, hanging on his every word as he described the pitfalls and privileges of his only-child existence. He elaborated on his mother's doting presence and her fair-haired loveliness, and, at Sasha's gently probing, he revealed that she had died tragically, at thirty, of a lingering illness.

"Thirty?" Sasha murmured. "My age?"

They lapsed into a silence which she ended with a soft question. "Was your father heartbroken?"

Marc didn't answer her right away. "That would have been difficult," he said. "He didn't have a heart."

She stared at him in the rebounding silence as though she knew they'd reached a door that wouldn't open.

"I'm sorry," she said at last.

He didn't respond. There wasn't time. An oddly familiar female voice interrupted his train of thought and sent a bullet of surprise through him.

"Marc?"

He turned, splashing water, and saw the smiling woman approaching them. His mental processes jammed. He knew the voice, but the unadorned face and the odd clothes didn't match. A wrinkled tunic top flowed to her calves, nearly covering the matching pants beneath it, and her hair was cropped short. It wasn't until she reached the edge of the Jacuzzi and crouched down that Marc put a name to the face. "Leslie?"

Leslie Parrish laughed and nodded. "How're you doing, Marc? Thought you might be worried about me."

"Worried? That doesn't quite cover it, Leslie. Where the hell have you been?"

"Back east."

"New York?"

She shook her head, still laughing softly. "No, a little farther east, actually. India. I've been studying higher forms of consciousness." She glanced briefly at Sasha and smiled. "Lovely girl, Marc. Your latest victim?"

•   •   •

"You're not really serious about Marc, are you?" Leslie queried later that same morning. Perched cross-legged on Sasha's bed, she could have been one of Shakespeare's weird sisters in a toga. "You *can't* be."

Stretched on her side on the floor, Sasha continued her leg raises. She'd been exercising off and on ever since Leslie arrived. Sasha always exercised when she was upset. "Why can't I?"

"Because he's so yang and you're so yin."

"And if I happen to like yang?" Sasha picked up the pace of her leg raises. "Besides, opposites attract," she said.

"Abbott and Costello were opposites," Leslie observed. "Look what happened to them."

"What happened to them?"

"I wasn't privy to the details, but they're not together any longer, are they?"

"They've both passed away, Leslie."

She shrugged. "There you go."

Sasha rolled onto her back and hoisted her legs in the air for some bicycling. Leslie's attempts to talk her out of a relationship with Marc might have made sense if Leslie had wanted him back for herself, but she didn't. She'd made that perfectly clear ten minutes after arriving. "I'm a different woman now, Marc," she'd told him. Rolling her pants above her knees, she'd dangled her feet in the Jacuzzi and smiled at them both. "My ego, I'm happy to say, is quiescent. Physical love and material gratification no longer have any hold on me."

She'd further informed them that she expected to return to India shortly, where she was studying under a famous swami and added that she'd come by only to pick up her things.

Her serene state of mind wasn't catching, apparently. Marc didn't seem to give a damn about her quiescent ego. He informed her that she'd breached a contract, and finally, in exasperation at her sublime lack of concern, he absented himself from the Jacuzzi and the deck. At that point Leslie had turned to Sasha with a commiserating smile. "Dear boy's a zero in the humor department, among *other* things."

Dropping her legs down, Sasha groaned and sprawled flat. She hadn't understood the reference at the time, but she was beginning to. Besides picking up her valuables, Leslie's mission, so far as Sasha could figure it out, was to save another woman from making the same mistake that she had made—falling in love with Marc Renaud.

Leslie's insistent voice broke through Sasha's recall. "You know, of course, that he's completely self-involved," Leslie warned. "Booze, cigs, and his films. Those are the only things he needs."

Sasha started on a round of scissor kicks. "I haven't found him to be that way at all," she said, hoping to discourage Leslie. "He's considerate and attentive. In fact, he's very sweet."

"*Sweet?* Give him time," Leslie prophesied gloomily. "He'll revert. The man is incapable of giving of himself on a sustained basis. Oh, don't get me wrong, I love him dearly, but he's unevolved."

Sasha sprang up, jogging in place. "I have to go run now," she announced.

"Don't you ever get tired?" Leslie asked.

Sasha spun and headed for the door. Tired? If Leslie didn't leave soon, she would need Bink, Arturo, and a stretcher to get from one room to the other.

•   •   •   •

Marc joined Sasha halfway through the run. She heard his rhythmic breathing and smiled as he jogged up alongside her.

"What's bugging Leslie?" he asked.

"She thinks you're unevolved."

"Really? Sounds terminal."

"I stood up for you," Sasha said, searching his intent profile. "I told her you were . . . sweet."

He glanced back, a quirk of ironic humor in his smile. "Sweet? Did she collapse laughing?"

"I don't think she bought it."

Their laughter lingered softly as they continued running, but the silence that eventually replaced it had a quality of uneasiness to it, as though neither knew quite what to say next, as though no subject seemed easy or safe enough to broach. Finally their deepened breathing was the only common sound. Sasha sensed that something was different between them, and it frightened her. Leslie's return was raising a barrier, not because Marc was still in love with Leslie, or her him. It was simply that any outside interference would have burst the bubble of enchantment that had surrounded them for the last few days. It was all too fragile and new, their relationship, their feelings for each other. Everything that had happened between them felt like a dream now that reality had intruded.

"Thank you," he said at last, "for standing up for me."

Without thinking what she was doing or why, Sasha veered out into the water, splashing through the surf that swished around her ankles.

Marc followed her, water flying as he claimed her wrist.

Her heart was beating wildly as she turned to him. "Was I right to stand up for you?" she asked.

"Was I, Marc?" The fear had become anxiety, a soft blockage in her throat.

He searched her eyes and his smile turned sad. "I guess I'm not very sweet when it comes right down to it, am I?"

She needed reassurance, and they both knew it. Leslie's warnings were all the more threatening because Sasha half believed they might be true. "She says you're incapable of giving, Marc."

"Sasha, don't—"

Still breathing heavily, Sasha avoided his eyes, but she couldn't stop herself. Her fears tumbled out in a flood of questions. "She made it sound as if you don't need anyone or anything, especially a relationship with someone like me. I told her she was wrong, Marc. Did I do the right thing?"

Marc went quiet as the surf crashed in around them. There was conflict in his grip on her wrist. There was the pain of a decision he didn't want to make in his eyes. "I don't know," he said at last. "I honestly don't know what I need at this moment."

Sasha could hardly breathe. He slackened his hold, and she pulled away. "That's not good enough," she said, her heart breaking a little with every word. "I can't defend a man who won't defend himself."

"Sasha—" He turned to the horizon, his voice catching with frustration, with a glint of the turmoil he harbored. "There are so many things you don't understand, dammit. You have this naïveté about life—"

"Then tell me, Marc, tell me about the things I don't understand."

He stared out at the water, his profiled face half shadowed. His eyes were pale and silvery in the light, more luminescent than she'd ever seen them.

They frightened her with their capacity to turn cold and distant, to shut out all human emotion? Was that what was happening now? Or was it a trick of the light? As she stared at him, her mind formed questions, painful, escalating questions. Why was he doing this, closing her out? Where was the man who had loved her so tenderly, the man who'd brought tears to her eyes with his anguish?

"Marc?" Something inside her went crazy with despair when he didn't answer. She broke away and began jogging back toward the beach house, her pulse shallow, her thoughts jumbling. When he made no attempt to follow her, she took it as the final rejection. It was over, all of it, the tenderness, the staggering passion—over and done with, wrapped like the movie.

As she reached the beach house, she tried to convince herself that she was overreacting, that it was the actress in her, the affinity for drama. But the feelings persisted, and finally a kind of desperation overtook her as she faced the possibility of losing the beauty that she and Marc had shared over the past few days. The thought was nearly unbearable.

By the time she reached her room and locked the door behind her, a searing spot of pain pierced her chest. It felt like an arrow through her heart. Corny, she thought, tears misting her eyes as she sank down on the bed, Lord, how unbelievably corny.

Sasha didn't see Marc or Leslie the rest of the day. That evening, lured by the aromatic smells of Arturo's cooking—and by a tiny, uncontrollable burgeoning of hope—she put in an appearance at dinner and found the two of them already in the dining room, drinking champagne. They were conversing quietly and seemed to have come to some kind of uneasy truce for which Sasha was grateful, although the sight of Marc with a half-empty champagne bottle in his hand made her throat tighten with sadness.

The spring lamb and mint sauce Arturo prepared were as delicious as the dinner conversation was disastrous. Sasha picked at her food as Marc gloomily finished off the champagne and Leslie discoursed on the dangers of red meat. Finally, as though he'd been cued, Arturo appeared at the door and announced that Marc had a phone call.

Daunted by Leslie's endlessly bright patter and mystical bent, Sasha was about to excuse herself when Marc reappeared in the doorway, a pack of cigarettes in his hand. He tapped one out, lit it, and took a long drag. There was something taut about him, a turbulence held in check.

"That was Paul Maxwell," he told Sasha, exhaling a blue jet of smoke. "The studio's found out that Leslie's back, and they don't want to take a chance on the press discovering that there are two of you. They want you out of here, Sasha. Tonight."

Sasha pulled a stack of panties from the dresser drawer and tossed them into her suitcase on the bed. They landed every which way, corners unfolding, colors mixing. Absently aware that she was desecrating Arturo's meticulous handiwork, she gave the patchouli sachet a heave next, and missed. Dunk shot needs some work, she thought.

Heartsick and confused, she glanced around her bedroom, at the moonlight glowing in the alcove, at the French provincial loveliness, and realized she couldn't leave yet. Not this way, not with so many things left unsaid. Peering in the direction of Marc's bedroom, she imagined him lying on his bed, chain-smoking Gauloises . . . and thinking about her?

She slammed shut the dresser drawer. He was thinking about her, undoubtedly, but not willing to talk to her and certainly not willing to explain himself. He'd made his excuses and left the dining room as soon as he'd passed on the studio's message. Apparently he wasn't even going to say good-bye.

Yanking the drawer open again, she grabbed another stack of underwear, walked to the case, and stared at it. With a tight sigh she unloaded the lingerie on the floor, adding to the heap that was already there, and turned to the wall that divided her bedroom from his. She couldn't do it like this, not on his terms. There was too much inside her, too much unexpressed. If he didn't want to talk, dammit, then he could listen.

He answered his door on the first knock. She didn't allow herself to think that he'd been waiting, though it was the first notion that entered her head as she accepted his invitation to come in. Her eyes were drawn to a ceramic ashtray by his bed, overflowing with cigarette butts. Aware of him behind her, she turned, met his crystalline gaze, and felt her heart wrench. There was something beautiful and desolate in his face. Something so near to hopelessness that she was gripped with a spasm of longing, shaken with it.

In the wake of that awareness, the emotion that flooded her was stunningly impassioned. *I love him*, she thought, shocked to her soul. *I do, I love him.* Her throat rasped painfully as she tried to clear away the gravelly sensations. It couldn't be true. She didn't want it to be true! The awful, messy, complicated prospect of loving him appalled her. But it was true, it was. She *was* in love with him.

He broke the silence finally, his voice irresistibly husky. "To what do I owe the honor?"

She blinked at the question. It took her a moment to realize that she was also angry with him, righteously angry, just-what-the-hell-are-your-intentions-fella angry. She walked to the ashtray, picked it up with trembling fingers, and dumped it in the wastebasket beside his bed. "What happened between us, Marc?" she asked.

"I don't know, a lot of things—"

She whirled around, eyes blazing. "Yes! Important things, passionate things, precious things. How can you discount those moments?"

"I'm not discounting anything. I know what happened between us." He walked across to the night table, picked up a pack of cigarettes, and found it empty. "All right, it was good, Sasha, is that what you wanted to hear? It was more than good, it was magnificent." He crushed the pack in his hand and lobbed it into the wastebasket. "And now it's over."

The arrow stabbed her again, piercing through Sasha's heart, twisting in the wound. "Over?" She breathed the word. "*Over?* You can discard it all so easily?"

He stared at her, his jaw muscles drawn tight over the bones of his face, his voice achingly flat. "Better that you know it now. Leslie was right about me. I'm not capable of giving."

"I don't believe that."

"Believe it, Sasha, because it gets worse. I don't give anything away, not unless I get something back for it, value for value. You had something I needed—a face, a body that resembled my missing star's." He raked a hand through his hair, rage and sadness in the rigid stroke of his arm. "The picture's done, Sasha, the party's over. Open those beautiful eyes, for God's sake, and read the fine print. Your services are no longer needed."

The look in his eyes told her more than his brutal words. He despised himself for what he was doing, for hurting her, but he would do it again if he had to, *if she made him.* Yes, he would hurt her again if she stayed.

She took a step back, her legs jerky, her hand grasping air as she tried to balance herself. He was giving her no choice but to leave.

Sasha could remember very little of what happened after that. She wasn't sure how she made it out of his room without coming apart, or into Bink's limo, but she did somehow. She took her leave of the Malibu beach house in silence, her mind numbed, her legs trembling, her dignity intact. It wasn't until she was halfway to Redondo Beach that she curled into a ball and sobbed.

Ten

"Pardon me, am I interrupting your coma?"

Slumped in a captain's chair at the juice bar, Sasha pulled out of her unfocused stare long enough to acknowledge the owner of the sardonic voice. It was T.C., and he had a handful of checks for her to sign.

"Make an X," he ordered, dropping the pile in front of her and shoving a pen into her writing hand.

She scribbled listlessly and pushed them back at him.

Obviously exasperated, he pulled his wheelchair up close to her. "What do I have to do to get your attention these days, McCleod? Call a press conference?" His voice dropped to a whisper. "You're bad for business, woman. You're depressing the customers. Hell, you're depressing *me*—wandering around like a lovesick kid and staring off into thin air."

Sasha tried to mask her misery with a smile that didn't quite come off. "Where's your compassion, T.C.?" she said with a sigh, "I'm suffering."

She went back to staring at the tumbler of juice du jour in front of her. She *was* suffering, keenly, though no one seemed to understand that. Apparently they thought the "boss lady" didn't hurt like other people.

"Suffering won't pay the bills, Camille," he muttered, rolling off in a huff. Sasha didn't even bother to glance after him. Poor T.C. She knew he was worried about her. She was worried too. She'd been back at The Fitness Factor a week, and she couldn't bring herself to get involved in anything. None of the activities that had brought her joy pre-Marc Renaud held any appeal for her now. She had no appetite, and when she forced herself to eat, she had trouble keeping the food down. She couldn't sleep for more than a couple of hours at a time.

She was obsessed.

She was wasting away, like Camille.

Impossible as it still seemed, she *was* in love.

At first, T.C. had tried to lure her back to normalcy with pep talks and swaggering dares like "Feelin' gutsy enough to take on the paper airplane king? Spot you a foot and a half." When none of that worked, he went straight to parental injunctions, and now he was trying to shame her out of the blues apparently. It was sweet of him really, she supposed. He cared, but nothing he or anyone else came up with put even the slightest dent in her depression. Didn't they understand she was inconsolable?

"Some people are destined to be together," she'd tried to tell T.C. her second day back. In her frustration, she'd picked unconvincing examples: Antony and Cleopatra, Charles and Diana, Mickey and Minnie. "All right, maybe not Charles and Diana," she'd admitted when he questioned her sanity, "but Marc Renaud and I *are* fated, I know it in my bones. I've never been so sure of anything in my life." She wouldn't hurt this way for someone she wasn't supposed to be with, would she? Sasha was too practical to believe that. She'd been heartsick since she'd left the beach house, that was all, *heartsick*. If the intensity of her pain didn't indicate romantic foreordainment, then what did?

Even when T.C. had dismissed her unshakable certainty as nonsense and smugly informed her that Antony and Cleopatra weren't a match made in heaven, either, she couldn't be dissuaded from believing that she and Marc were soulmates.

It wasn't at all like Sasha to be self-indulgent or self-pitying. She disliked those traits, considered them character flaws, in fact, but she couldn't seem to help herself. She'd lost control of her car somewhere along the bumpy road of life. She was drifting through her days in a trance, uncaring and uninvolved, and it looked as though she might go on that way indefinitely. . . .

Fortunately, life had something more interesting in store for Sasha. She was to languish only two more days before an unexpected event jolted her back to reality.

The event was the arrival of Leslie Parrish. When the ex–movie star walked into The Fitness Factor late one muggy, listless afternoon, Sasha could hardly believe her eyes. "Leslie?" she said, staring at the woman with whom she shared two things in common, a physical resemblance and Marc Renaud. If ever she'd seen a bearer of bad news, Sasha thought, interpreting the actress's frantic wave as a harbinger of trouble.

Leslie flew across the room, drew Sasha out of the captain's chair, hugged her forcefully, and stepped back. "I'm so glad I found you, Sasha," she said. "It's about Marc."

Sasha's heart nearly tripped over itself. "What's wrong?"

"Can we talk?" Glancing around to see who might be listening, Leslie sank down into a chair at Sasha's table and waited until Sasha did the same. "They're screaming at the studio," she confided. "Marc hasn't exercised his final cut option on the film, and he and Paul Maxwell got into it the other night. Before it was over, Marc told Paul pretty graphically what he could do with the movie *and* Gemini Studios." She threw up her hands. "I swear, Sasha, he doesn't seem to care about anything these days."

It was the best news Sasha had heard all week. "Tell me more."

"He looks terrible. He's drinking too much—" Leslie peered at her, scrutinizing. "You don't look too terrific yourself. You're thin, you're pale—"

"I'm fine, Leslie," Sasha cut in. "I had a touch of the flu, that's all."

"Umm, just as I thought," Leslie said, slowly tapping a finger to her lips. "You're not eating I'll bet, or sleeping either. It's him, isn't it?" She sighed. "It's criminal the effect that man has on women!"

"Let's turn him into the love police," Sasha suggested darkly.

Leslie gave her a commiserating smile. "Not a half-bad idea, but let's take care of you first. There's a whole truckload of hurt under that sarcasm, girl, admit it. You're pining. Listen, if it's any comfort to you, he's crazy in love with you too. Either that, or he's gone completely over the edge."

"Crazy in love? Marc?" Sasha slid forward in the chair. "Are you certain? Oh, my Lord," she

murmured at Leslie's firm nod. "I knew it." She
looked around for her office manager. Maybe he
would believe her now. "T.C.!"

"Shhhh," Leslie said, pulling her chair up to the
table. "Don't get carried away. We've got to talk
first. You have no idea what a mess you're letting
yourself in for."

"I know he's difficult, but—"

"Difficult? Open your eyes, child. He's downright self-destructive." Leslie was suddenly serious. "You knew he was the son of a marquis,
didn't you?"

"Yes, why?"

"Did you also know his father was dead?"

Sasha remembered Paul Maxwell mentioning
something about Marc's father. She nodded again,
hesitantly. Something in Leslie's frown told her
this wasn't fun and games anymore.

Leslie glanced around the juice bar and returned
her gaze to Sasha as though trying to decide how
much she should reveal. "I probably shouldn't do
this," she admitted, her voice hushed, "but before
you do something you'll regret, there are things
you have to know about Marc Renaud. He has a
past tragic enough to destroy the average person.
I don't know all the details, but it has to do with
his childhood—a love/hate thing with his father,
his mother's death."

"I guess it was a couple of years ago," she went
on, her breath gathering in a sigh. "I'd been shooting at night, location stuff on the remake of a
fifties mystery thriller, a Hitchcockian thing. Anyway, I came home late that night, near midnight,
and found Marc roaring drunk. The beach house
was in a shambles, and he kept ranting about
'the old man.' I finally realized it was the anniver-
sary of his father's death. I wish now that I hadn't

kept after him the way I did. I begged him to tell me what was wrong."

"And he did?"

"Yes . . . he finally admitted that he'd been in a terrible fight with his father the night the old man died. He said he was responsible for his father's death. He hadn't been able to stop him from shooting himself."

"When did this happen?" Sasha asked, her voice faint with shock.

"The shooting? I guess it must be nearly five years ago. I met him a year later, at the Cannes Film Festival. He was just coming out of a bout of depression and drinking. 'His walk in the wilderness,' the gossip columnists called it. They assumed he was grieving for his father. Apparently no one knew what a monster the old man was—except the immediate family." She sank back in the couch. "The rich and their secrets."

Sasha couldn't respond. Her mind was hurtling back, recollecting the signs she'd seen in him, the anguish, the staggering, tortured passion when he'd made love to her. She'd never imagined a man could make love the way he did, as though his sanity, even his life had depended on it. She had to go to him, she thought. She had to help him.

When she looked up, Leslie was shaking her head as though she knew what Sasha was thinking. "Don't, Sasha, you won't change anything, I know. I love him, too, in my way, but he's been too badly damaged by this thing. Listen to me, you can't help him now."

No, she *could* help him, Sasha knew. She could be what he needed. She was what he needed.

"Sasha, please, listen to me. You're the first person he's allowed himself to care about since it happened. Without realizing it, you've opened wounds. He needs to struggle with the guilt by himself. For both your sakes, let him be."

But Sasha wasn't listening. In her mind she was reliving the rehearsal when he'd kissed her with such savage tenderness and ripped her dress in his anguish. He'd told her he would die without her. That hadn't been Jesse; it had been Marc Renaud talking to her. Leslie was wrong. He did need her. She was the only one who *could* help him.

"Tell T.C. I was called away," Sasha said, heedless of Leslie's cautioning voice as she rose out of the chair. Negotiating a single-minded arc through her small office, she whisked her shoulder bag off the coat tree and headed for the door.

"Sasha, wait—"

The four-letter word that followed Sasha into the hallway evaporated in a sigh of resignation. "Who's T.C.?" Leslie called after her.

No one answered Sasha's insistent knock at the front gate of the beach house. Driven by emotions that wouldn't allow her to listen to reason, she paced along the seven-foot block wall, searching for a way to get over and oblivious of the traffic racing along the coastal highway. Finally, a quarter mile down the road, she found an entrance to one of the public beaches that dotted the waterfront. If she doubled back, she could get to Marc's place from the beach.

The ocean was swallowing up the sun as she came upon his house at last, its glass facade aflame with the brilliant crimson and violet hues of dusk. Sasha paused a moment, struck by the infernolike beauty. In mythology fire was often a symbol, not just of death but of renewal, the end or the beginning. Which was this, she wondered.

Leslie's warning came back to her as she took the steps that led up to the deck off the kitchen, and for the first time a flash of doubt intruded on her thoughts. Could she help him? Was it possible for someone to be beyond the healing touch of love? The mild onshore breeze suddenly felt chill against her back. What if he rejected her?

She found the glass doors unlocked and the kitchen in total disarray—empty bottles of wine, leftover food, crushed cigarette packs. It looked much the way she'd found his inner sanctum the day she'd arrived. The urge to clean up the chaos shimmered through her, and now, oddly, she saw the inherent value in such an act. People needed order in their lives, and discipline. There was sanity in discipline. There was direction and purpose. She could bring those things to his life, she thought. She could help him.

She found him in his room, seated in an antique chair in front of the open patio doors and staring out at the twilight's consuming fire. Her impulses were at war. He looked so quiet, so pulled into himself. Did she dare disturb him?

Finally. "Marc?"

He swung around in the chair and stared at her with eyes that had not lost any of their ability to turn her soul inside out. Pale and harrowingly beautiful, they pierced her defenses and ripped right through her heart. She drew in a breath through her nostrils that made her dizzy. When she spoke, her voice shook. "Are you all right?"

His mouth tightened, white at the edges.

She felt lost and frightened in that moment, unsure what his reaction meant.

Hunching forward in the intensifying silence,

he held his head in his hands. "I've missed you," he said finally, simply, murmuring the words into the loose cradle of his palms. And then he looked up at her.

When she spoke her voice broke, and she took a halting, painful step forward. "I missed you too."

He held out his arms, and she flew at him, dropping into his lap, a wild cry of relief and joy rioting through her.

"Sasha," he said with a groan, his voice butchered by emotion. He crushed her in the explosive power of his embrace, sending tremors through the ancient chair's wooden frame as they rocked and sighed and shuddered. The passion that overtook them, that drove them together, was pure and soul-shattering. It was ecstasy tinged with anguish.

Sasha broke away, needing to look at him, to see if the amazing burst of love she felt was there in his brilliant eyes. Racked with his own need, Marc brought her back, barely in control of the near-violent emotion inside him. He was wild with urges, crazy to hold her, devour her, become a part of her body.

She was an exquisite, quivering thing in his arms, sobbing and gasping out her happiness. She was an angel of redemption, *his angel.* Her breasts brushed his arms, and desire burned through his psyche, scorching away pain and guilt, freeing him of everything but a raging need to know her naked softness again—her skin, her scent, the ravishing sweetness of her. She was life itself. She was the warm, drizzly wild honey that made his loins throb and his jaws ache with pleasure.

He took her parted lips in a kiss that was agonizingly slow and deep in its penetration, primal in its urgency. His tongue plunged into the vault of her mouth, skimming her teeth, skirting the tender chamber of her throat. Sasha was helpless, a whimpering child as he slowly withdrew it and tantalized her lips with feathery strokes. She groaned with pleasure, arching instinctively as he began to coax her tongue into the silky heat of his own mouth.

At first she resisted the suction pulling her in, and then, aware of his index finger caressing the corner of her lips, she let herself be drawn deeper into him. His sharp shudder thrilled her. His body tensed. She could even feel him hardening beneath her. She darted her tongue into his mouth again and again with a throaty moan.

She whispered yes as he unfastened the buttons on her cotton cardigan. Releasing the front hook of her bra, he cupped her breasts in his hands and took the tip of one creamy mound into his mouth. He stroked her flushed skin with his tongue, sucking her gently, roughly, as his need burgeoned.

"Your body, this sweetness"—his voice was a groan of pleasure—"it's tearing me apart."

She burned under his lips, her breasts swollen, her nipples cresting with sensation. Desire was a living, flaring thing inside her, as powerful and consuming as the flames of sunset outside the doors.

"There's only one thing on earth I want right now." He pressed his palm into the valley between her pelvic bones. "*This*. This tight, silky miracle around me."

Before she knew what was happening, he was turning her, bringing her body around until she straddled him on the chair. His hands slid up her widespread legs, peeling back her skirt until her thighs and lace panties were exposed. With one deft movement, he undid his jeans and released the rigid heat between his legs.

Sasha's head swam dizzily at the sight of him. Her body melted and ran like butter left in the sun. The magnificent need in his body, in his face, was overwhelming. Sweetly shocked and utterly aroused, she felt a trembling gush of desire. The liquid fire, the aching tenderness at the juncture of her thighs, made her sharply aware of her body's needs. Deep muscles contracted, clutching against their own emptiness. Sweet Lord, but she wanted that hardened splendor moving deeply inside her, thrilling her, filling her up until she was bursting with him.

"I'm aching for you," she whispered, flushing at her own boldness as she touched him.

Marc pulled aside the obstruction of her panties and drew her onto him. Sasha cried out with pleasure as he surged into her, thrusting as deeply as her body would allow. He gripped her hips, holding her still when she began to rock and undulate with the enchanting rhythms that beat in her loins. An instant later he released her, and she arched up, moving with the guidance of his hands, moaning, crying out again as he brought her back down.

Sasha moved under his hands like a woman possessed, flowing with desire, crazed with the wild, engorging pleasure he gave her. As she felt the ecstasy building, she lost the cadence of her beautiful, sinuous dance to the quick rhythms of completion. She was sobbing with the pure, undiluted joy of it, nearly insensate with pleasure.

Marc felt as though a hot, golden sun were pulsating around him. All the energy in his body flowed to the spot that she was caressing with her body. Every cell of his consciousness centered there as the sun gathered radiance and swelled to bursting with the intensity of its own brilliance.

Sasha heard him force out a guttural cry that sounded like her name. He swept her into his arms and crushed her to him ardently. Yes, it *was* her name he was repeating hoarsely and with such passion it brought an aching lump to her throat.

"Sasha," he said in a raspy voice, "Sasha, Sasha . . ."

She bathed in the sound and swayed with the bursts of his muscles, her own body spasming softly until she was nearly spent with stimulation.

Their heated, heartstrung sounds mingled with the soft rumble of the ocean below and the beautiful, mournful creak of the old chair beneath them. Beyond that there was only the depth and silence of the evening sky as it spun out its music, the velvet dusk as melody, the emerging stars as grace notes.

In the quiet that followed, Sasha was struck with a sense of unfurling possibilities, as though everything needed and desired were within reach. She held off for as long as she could, and then, still full of emotion, she took his face in her hands and whispered to him gently. "Marc, it's going to be all right, all of it, I promise you. Leslie told me," she explained, "I know—"

His eyes registered a glint of shock. Catching hold of her hand, he squeezed it. "What did Leslie tell you? What do you know, Sasha?"

With his body still deeply inside her, she was too jubilant, too full of joy and love to pay attention to the warning signals in his eyes. "She told me about your father," she said, caressing the tousled hair from his forehead. "She told me everything—and it's all right. Really, Marc, please believe me. It *is* all right."

He closed his eyes and exhaled. Finally, cursing softly, he took her hands from his face and held them between his. "Sasha, you don't know what you're saying. It's not all right."

"No, you're wrong." She smiled, even laughed a little at the absurdity of his comment. Didn't he know that nothing he'd done could change her mind about him now or quell the emotion she felt? "Everything's going to be fine. And do you know why? Because I love you, Marc. That's why. I love you."

His throat caught painfully in a swallow, and his body reacted with a physical flinch.

"What's wrong?" she cried as he cupped the back of her head and brought her to him, hugging her so fiercely that she was instantly frightened. Without a word of explanation he released her and grasped her hips, lifting her from the heat of him.

A moment later Sasha stood on shaky legs, awkwardly pulling her skirt down and fumbling with the buttons on her sweater. Speechless, she watched him walk out onto the deck and stand at the railing. His name was on her lips, but she didn't have enough breath inside her to voice it. It seemed a long time before she could move. Empty and chilled, she walked to the threshold.

He turned at the sound of her movement, his eyes dulled with the burden of unwanted memories. "Leslie shouldn't have told you," he said, "but since she did, you might as well know it all. I wanted my father dead, the brutal bastard. He drove my mother into her grave with his insane rantings and ravings, his jealousies, his delusions."

He folded his arms and began to walk, talking

in a low, abstracted voice. "When I left the estate on my eighteenth birthday, he threatened to disown me. I had defied his direct order to restore the estate to its former glory. It didn't matter that the soil had gone bad years before and the buildings were in crumbling disrepair. It didn't matter that I loathed the place, and him. . . ."

He hesitated a moment, listening to the distant cry of gulls. "Five years ago, when I learned through his lawyers that he was gravely ill, I made the mistake of agreeing to go to see him. They told me he was dying, that he wanted to make amends. Actually he had something very different in mind." He turned to her, his eyes dark in the fading light. "He pulled a gun. He threatened to kill himself if I didn't assume my place as heir to the title and lands. It was the final, the ultimate manipulation."

Turning back to the water, he shut her out. "He put the gun to his head, and I tried to stop him." His next words were barely audible. "The gun went off."

Sasha felt a terrible taste rise in her throat. It was horror and shock. It was sadness for him. "I'm sorry, Marc, about all of it, everything that happened. Please believe me. But none of that matters now, not to me. I love you."

She heard him sigh, and the sound was unbearably sad to her ears. The arrowlike pain struck again, piercing her heart with such ferocity she thought it would never end. "Marc?" she asked, thoroughly frightened, "did you hear me? I said I love you."

When he turned back she saw that he had heard. The sadness was riveting in his pale blue irises, but there was a shading of something cruel beneath it, as though his pain were too great for him not to lash out.

"Are you so sure that it's love, Sasha? Have you ever thought it might be more complicated than that, like the fact that I'm broken and need fixing, for example?"

She shook her head, confused, wanting him to stop.

"I saw it the first moment you walked on that stage, weeks ago," he persisted, his voice harsh, "the crusader complex. You have this thing about righting wrongs, defending the underdog. You even took me on when I yelled at Jimmy. So what's the attraction, Sasha? Do you have some crazy need to save me from myself? Is that it?"

"No! No, of course not."

"Lost soul? Isn't that what you called me? Weren't those your exact words?"

'Yes, but I didn't mean—"

Beneath his anger the sadness flared again. "It doesn't matter, Sasha. It doesn't matter what your motives are. I'm going back."

"Back?"

"To France."

"When? For how long?" Her voice dropped to a whisper. "Why?"

"I have to. I haven't been back since it happened."

Everything else he might have said was there in his face. He had ghosts in his homeland, excoriating memories to be faced, and emotions to purge. "For how long?" Desperation crept into her voice. "You'll be back?"

His jaw flexed as he shook his head. "The studio has some things for me to do over there, a film festival, scouting locations . . . I'll be gone a few months."

The arrow turned like a knife blade in her heart.

How could he do this? She knew he was emotionally savaged, that he had to go back, that he might never be ready for a relationship, but she didn't care about any of that. She was balanced precariously on the razor's edge of her own pain. She cared nothing for his anguish in that moment, only that he was hurting her. Lord, how he was hurting her.

"All right," she said finally, her voice shaking with outrage. "All right, then, you do what you have to. You go—for a few months—whatever. But know this, *know this*!" She caught hold of the gold heart around her neck, and her voice twisted with sadness. "I do love you, Marc Renaud. I will always love you. However you may choose to rationalize that fact, you're going to have to live with the knowledge that someone cared about you once—bastard that you are!—really cared about you. And you ran from her."

She turned, fighting tears, and fled the room.

Eleven

For Sasha the next several days swept by in a blur of hurt and hell-hath-no-fury indignation. "Well, it's better than Camille, isn't it?" she said to T.C. one morning when he complained that she was slamming file drawers and banging around his office like a cat with its tail in a knot.

"Camille was quiet at least," he observed.

Sasha rifled through folders looking for copies of a liability insurance rider that was about to expire. She came up empty-handed, turned to T.C., and sent the file drawer careening shut with a bump of her hip.

"Camille was a jerk," she said bitterly. "I mean, let's face it—a lingering death over some guy who wasn't worth a bout of the twenty-four-hour flu? No siree, not for this kid, no more of that dying-on-the-vine nonsense for me. There's not a man on the planet worth that kind of grief."

T.C.'s sigh was heavy. "Sasha," he offered patiently, "don't you think it's time we had a heart-to-heart? Tell ol' Top Cat all about it, okay? You'll feel better, and there'll be less wear and tear on the office furniture. Besides, I'm curious. What actually went wrong with you and Renaud, anyway?"

In no mood for a heart-to-anything, Sasha shook her head. Like a romantic fool, she had half hoped Marc would postpone his trip to Europe and come after her when she rushed out of the beach house, or at least call her before he left. With every day that had gone by, she'd died a little, waiting. Finally, mercifully, she had gotten angry, very, *very* angry.

"Thanks, T.C., but no thanks."

She snagged a nail banging the next drawer, and, paradoxically, the mishap nearly undid her. "Damn, damn, *damn!*" she said with a moan, shaking her finger. The ragged tear brought her no physical pain, but the suddenness, the unfairness, the sheer defeat of it sent her blood pressure skyrocketing. Her throat filled with outrage over life's little indignities. Over its huge inequities. Who arranged it so that what one wanted most in life was always unattainable, she wondered. Who did that?

She held on to the drawer and forced down the stinging upsurge of emotion. She would not lose control again over that man, *she would not!* Shaking with relief as the impulses passed, she turned to T.C.'s concerned gaze and saw what she'd been doing to him over the past few days. He looked confused, almost helpless in the face of her crisis. His silence made her realize how self-involved she'd become, and how blessed she was to have him for a friend. He'd not only put up with her, he'd stuck by her. "I guess I've been pretty miserable to be around lately, haven't I?"

His diffident shrug said it's okay, compadre, you're entitled. "If you change your mind about talking, my rates are reasonable."

"I'm going to be all right, T.C." she said, compressing her lips into a smile that promised him she would be.

The next few weeks slipped by quickly as Sasha worked diligently to make good on her promise. She resumed teaching her exercise classes and organized a racquetball tournament. With the check she received from Gemini Studios, she paid off the balloon mortgage payment and began plans to expand the juice bar into an intimate, on-site health food restaurant.

The hardest thing to put behind her was her sense of destiny with Marc Renaud. Some small part of her mind refused to relinquish its stubborn belief in a cosmic link. Maybe she did have the savior complex he'd accused her of. Or maybe their moment in time had come and gone, played itself out like a dust devil in the desert. Those were the reasons she gave herself, and since she had no other explanations for destiny's capriciousness, they had to do.

Sasha kept busy, but she needed something besides her work to occupy her, a distraction, a challenge. Surprisingly, it was Leslie Parrish who was to provide that distraction. The former actress had taken to stopping by the health club several times a week, ostensibly to work out, but Sasha noticed she was spending an unusual amount of time with T.C. Once Sasha even came upon T.C. giving Leslie a wheelchair tour of the facility. On his lap!

When she queried T.C. about it later, he merely winked. "She says I'm an old soul. You know, evolved."

Sasha laughed, really laughed, for the first time in weeks. "Oh, T.C., I don't believe it! You and Leslie?"

He almost blushed. "Hey, she likes deep thinkers, what can I say? I'm her idea of a macho dude, spiritually speaking." He wheeled off, humming a happy tune.

Sasha was delighted but apprehensive. T.C. and *Leslie*?

Fortunately Leslie brought up the subject herself after an afternoon aerobics class. She and Sasha were in the locker room, changing into street clothes, when Leslie began to wax philosophic about the male gender.

"Where men are concerned," she told Sasha, "there's a high road and a low road. I should know, I've logged plenty of miles in the passes. One day my memoirs will tell it all—how my best years were spent on a collision course with the wrong guys—actors, producers, *directors*," she added pointedly.

"Where does T.C. fit on your street map?" Sasha inquired.

Leslie raised an eyebrow and smiled. "That darlin' boy is definitely a viaduct on the turnpike of life. He's wonderful, isn't he?" she said, her smile turning secretive. "A woman bumps fenders with a guy like that maybe once in a lifetime."

Sasha nodded, her thoughts bittersweet. Yes, she knew all about that collision-of-a-lifetime feeling.

Leslie never gave her a chance to express her thoughts. If she was convinced that T.C. was an overpass, she was just as adamant that Marc Renaud was a tunnel. "You're better off without him, Sasha," she insisted. "I know you don't believe that yet, but one day you'll see I'm right."

As it turned out, Leslie was right on both counts. No, Sasha didn't believe her. And yes, that day of reckoning Leslie spoke of did come . . . exactly two months later, and in a manner that even Leslie wouldn't have expected.

Sasha just happened to be crouched by the edge of The Fitness Factor's Jacuzzi checking the water temperature when the phone call came. T.C.'s voice blasted through the pool's loudspeaker, nearly jolting her headfirst into the water.

"Gemini Studios!" he yelled. "Sasha, get in here!"

Sasha's nervous system reacted with a power surge that left her immobilized and trembling. Gemini? No, she told herself, it couldn't be Marc. Her thirty-second dash to the office felt like a marathon. Her legs were Jell-O as she took the phone receiver from T.C. and pressed her hand over the mouthpiece. "Who is it?" she whispered to T.C.

"Maxwell," he mouthed.

She faltered for a second, biting back her disappointment. "Paul?" Her voice sharpened in her effort to sound bright as she put the phone to her ear.

To her complete surprise, Paul Maxwell was bubbling over with good news. After thanking her warmly for all her "fine work" in the movie, he told her the studio was genuinely enthusiastic about the final cut of *Tell Me No Lies.* "We may have a minor masterpiece on our hands," he said. "We've accelerated the post-production process to get the film into the theaters before the summer rush. You should be seeing our publicity campaign in a matter of days."

But the crux of his call, it soon became apparent, was a warning. "I hope you haven't forgotten our agreement, Sasha. If word gets out that you were involved, we're taking the official position that you were a stand-in. You did a few long shots, action shots, nothing more. That should be your position as well, of course."

"Of course." Her voice was toneless as she wondered what she was going to do when the picture came out. Seeing it was out of the question. Even a glimpse of the clips on television would be an excruciating reminder of everything she'd been trying to forget. "What do you hear from Marc?" she asked, regretting the question as soon as it was out.

"Marc?" Paul's sigh was low and exasperated. "Who knows? We're lucky to make contact once a month—and then we have to track him down. . . ."

Seconds later, staring at the phone she'd just hung up, Sasha wondered numbly if she'd said goodbye. The memory of her last encounter with Marc flooded her, and suddenly she was clinging to him again, swaying with him in the antique chair, whispering his name. Her throat tightened, and tears stung her eyes. She turned and walked out of the office without another word to anyone and went straight to her car.

Once in her apartment, she began cleaning, the range first, then the refrigerator. The phone rang several times, stopping abruptly, starting again. She ignored it and poured on the elbow grease. It didn't matter a fig that the kitchen was virtually spotless. Cleaning was *action.* It was movement. It took the deliberate use of her brain to decide whether a liquid cleanser or a chlorine-based powder was the agent of choice for catsup stains. It forestalled what frightened her most—sinking back into the pit it had taken her months to crawl out of.

The phone rang again.

Her stampede into the kitchen ended with a choked, helpless cry as she stared at the bleating machine. "What is it?" she blurted out, grabbing up the phone.

"Sasha?" Lou Ryan's raspy voice assaulted her nerves.

"Oh, Lou, not *now,*" she said.

"Not now? What's that supposed to mean, not *now*? I've got the role of a lifetime for you! Listen to me, it's a star vehicle for Paramount—*Paramount*, Sasha—but there's just one catch. These guys want a name actress, a rising star."

"Then why are you calling me, Lou?" Sasha felt a wrench of regret for the childhood dream that would never be realized. She was never going to be a star, rising or otherwise, that much was certain.

"Haven't you heard? Word is out that *Tell Me No Lies* is fabulous. If we could convince the Gemini people to let you go public, imagine the publicity! Marc Renaud's mystery woman! Sasha? You there?? This is a window of opportunity situation. *Sasha?*"

Marc Renaud's mystery woman? Star? The labels buzzed raucously in her head, reminding Sasha that this was how it had all started, with a call from Lou Ryan. She'd hung up on him then—and made the mistake of picking up the phone the next time it rang.

"Good-bye, Lou," she said, her aim deadly as she hooked the phone in its cradle. She wouldn't make *that* mistake again.

Tell Me No Lies was a smash hit when it premiered two weeks later. Quietly amazed at the rave reviews and around-the-block lines at the theaters, Sasha didn't know what to think about it all. She was sad. She was proud. She was overwhelmed, especially by the fact that the critics were most ecstatic about her performance. They'd called the action shots "spellbinding," the love scene "hauntingly torrid" and "ineffably beautiful." Of course, they thought they were reviewing Leslie, but Sasha knew who had done the work, and the Gypsy child in her blossomed under the affirmations that it was good.

Lou Ryan sent her flowers and besieged her with phone calls. "Please, Sasha, go public! It'll put us both on the map!"

Sasha firmly refused. Beyond her agreement with Gemini, she had her own code of honor. She would never break a promise for reasons as self-serving as personal gain. Nevertheless, the pull of bright lights and poignant memories was strong in the days to come. Though it brought her pain, she found herself watching the trailers that ran on television and poring over the reviews. Every day she teetered on the brink of actually going to see the movie, standing in line, sitting in the theater, *crying her heart out.* No, she couldn't do it.

She'd nearly waited out the run of the film when she found herself home early one evening guiltily thumbing through the entertainment section of the newspaper. The television talk show she always watched droned in the background as she dunked fresh vegetables in yogurt dip and perused the movie listings. There was a seven o'clock showing she could still make. To go or not to go??? In the midst of her dilemma, a voice drifted through her consciousness.

". . . And after a word from our sponsors, we'll be right back for a chat with the director of *Tell Me No Lies.*"

Sasha spun around to the television in confusion. Director? They couldn't have meant director. He was an entire continent away. Producer maybe? Or star? She stared at the screen, adrenaline rousing her heart as the commercial came to an end and the show's lead-in theme began.

The announcer said it again, the D word—director!—and Sasha's senses reeled. The hostess's smiling face materialized, but Sasha couldn't make out a word of her introduction. All she could do was stare, transfixed. Forgetting to breathe, losing every lucid thought in her head, she followed the camera's pan to the woman's first guest: Marc-André Renaud?

Yes! Sasha gripped the back of the chair she was sitting in. Yes, it *was* him! He was smack on the screen in her own kitchen, every stunning inch of him, making his entrance, shaking the woman's hand, taking a seat next to her. As the camera focused in on his features, on his melancholy smile and wrenchingly beautiful gaze, Sasha felt a soft spasm of pain. She lifted her head and clenched her jaw, stubbornly fighting the sensation.

In the first few seconds of his polite exchange with the hostess, Sasha nearly died hearing his voice. Would she ever get over him? *Ever?* Such a flare of anguish filled her heart that she curled a fist in the hollow of her throat. Her other hand found the remote control on the kitchen table. She couldn't watch. She would have to turn the television off. It came to her then, as she was about to hit the button and send him into oblivion, that she was staring at the man who had ruined her, destroyed her . . . *saved her.* Wasn't she better for having known him? Wasn't she stronger? Didn't the pain purify her in some way and give her more compassion?

Her finger hovered over the button as the hostess asked her first question. "Did you come back to promote your movie, Mr. Renaud?"

"No, actually," he said, "I came back to set the record straight."

The camera flashed briefly to the hostess's surprised expression before returning to Marc.

"The movie's getting excellent reviews," he explained, "and nobody could be happier about that than I. I just want to be sure that credit is given where credit is due. There's someone who deserves to take a bow for those reviews right alongside the rest of us who were involved. She's an excellent actress who came into the project at a difficult time—"

Sasha's hand froze.

"Are you saying it was intentional that she wasn't given credit?" the hostess broke in.

"Not intentional exactly, but we had to replace the star before several key scenes were completed. Luckily we found an actress whose resemblance to Leslie Parrish was so remarkable that we could finish the film. It was my decision to keep that actress's identity a secret. It's my decision now to give her the recognition she deserves for her work."

As a freeze-frame shot of Sasha running toward the water filled the screen, Marc's voice captioned, "You're looking at Sasha McCleod, the actress who did all the action shots and the critically acclaimed love scene."

"Mr. Renaud, this is something of a bombshell," the hostess said. "How does the studio feel about what you're doing?"

A faint smile crinkled his mouth. "I guess I'll find out after this show, won't I?"

"So you're doing this without their knowledge?"

"You could say that."

Sasha was nearly ill with astonishment. He was risking his position with the studio in order to give her credit? She stood, less out of reflex than to make sure that she could. Her mind rushed over the reasons he might be doing such a thing— guilt, a sense of obligation, personal publicity— but the only explanation that registered on her bewildered psyche was that he still cared. A man didn't jeopardize his career over casual feelings.

The hostess continued with probing questions about Sasha and the movie until Marc announced that he'd volunteered all the information he could. Adroitly heading her off with anecdotes about the location scouting he'd been doing in Europe, he steered the conversation to his latest project. The woman was polite throughout, but doggedly persistent with gossipy tidbits, and before the segment was over, she'd delved into Marc's personal life.

"I've been out of circulation for a few months now," Marc offered.

"I see. Giving up the vices, are we? Wine, women, and song?"

Marc shook his head amiably. "Song, maybe." He held his hand up, exaggerating the shakiness in his fingers. "I did give up smoking though." His tone was wry, pained, a man sorely tested. "Haven't had a cigarette in months."

He'd given up smoking? Sasha sank back down in the chair, her head spinning with the ramifications of that incredible bit of news. He'd quit *smoking*? Entranced, she wanted to hug the television, kiss the screen. For her, she wondered, her mind leaping once more to the only possible conclusion for a woman in her state of delirium. He did that for *her*?

She had to see him was the next impulse that mobilized her. Where was he? How would she find him? What were the call letters of that television station? Thoughts Ping-Ponged through her head, but some tiny inkling of reality held her in place. *Whoa*, she thought, skidding to a mental halt and scrambling to get back into the realm of logical possibilities. She wasn't just leaping to conclusions, she was pole-vaulting to them.

What if he didn't want to see her, she thought, alerted by a little bell ringing insistently in her head. What if his motive *were* guilt or obligation? What if Lou Ryan had contacted him? Her enthusiasm drooped. Suddenly the ringing in her head was drowned out by pounding. Someone was at her front door.

She wasn't sure what she said when she opened it and saw Marc there—or if she said anything at all. The single bell had become a thousand pealing chimes, doorbells, alarm bells, wind crystals, all singing out a beautiful chorus of sheer astonishment and sweet, wild hope. It was him. Breathing the same fragrant spring air she was. He was smiling faintly, gazing down at her.

Her throat swelled to bursting.

It came to her eventually, as she stared at him with a splash of a smile, that she was also pointing at the television where his interview had gone off only seconds before. "How did you get here so quickly?"

"I taped it this morning," he explained, his blue gaze capturing hers. "I'm glad you saw it, Sasha. I was hoping you would."

His voice was husky, the undercurrents so rich with resonance, she could have floated on them. "Are you going to be in trouble now?" she asked. "With the studio?"

"It wouldn't be anything new, would it? I'm always in trouble with the studio."

He moved into the room, and somehow she felt his fingers graze the inside of her wrist and enclose it in the heat of his hand.

"Sasha," he was saying, his voice caressing every letter in her name, "I want you to go to the movies with me. I think you're going to like the one I've got in mind. There's this incredibly beautiful woman and this moody, pain-in-the-neck guy who makes her life a living hell."

"A movie?" she whispered, hardly able to keep from flinging herself at him. "Why do you think I'd like it?"

"Because it has a happy ending."

"Really?"

"It's kind of a universal theme . . . troubled guy gets his life straightened out with a woman's help. Circumstances split them up, but he finally sees the light . . . and hopes it's not too late."

All she could do was shake her head and gasp as he swept her into his arms. "Marc," she cried softly, tangling her arms around his neck, pressing herself to him.

"Sasha," he said with a groan, "Sasha, I'm sorry. I had to go back. I had to deal with it alone, do you understand?" He brought her face up, kissed her eyes. "You were right, I was running. I had to go back and face my father's death, the guilt, the nightmares, or I would have kept running, from everything . . . *from you.*"

Tears streamed down her face as she pushed back to look at him. The sadness, the rage, were gone. The lights in his eyes were shimmering with heat and passion, the sweet, crazy need of a man for a woman. The touch of his hand on her waist made her ache for him. "Maybe we can go to a late show?" she suggested.

"You read minds too?" He pulled her closer, pressed his lips to her temple. "Did I tell you that in the movie the guy falls in love with the girl and asks her to marry him?"

"What's her answer?"

"She turns him down."

"What?"

His voice dissolved in a soft groan and his eyes

flared with desire as he picked her up and swung around with her in his arms, eyeing the living room couch. "She turns him down, which forces him to make mad, passionate love to her until she changes her mind."

Sasha gasped, laughing and crying as he lowered her to the couch. "And does he? Change her mind, I mean?"

"Yes," he said, his eyes full of fire and tenderness, "but it takes him a long, long time, because she's an amazingly strong-willed woman."

Sasha arched up to meet his mouth, her body already melting. "Strong-willed, but very shrewd," she murmured.

It was almost too late in the game when she asked him, too late for a sane question, a reasonable answer. She was so drugged with passion, she barely cared what his answer was going to be, but curiosity, the tenacious little voice that was and had always been her bête noire, made her ask. "Why did you do it, Marc? Why did you put your career at risk for mine?"

His eyes were suddenly serious. He touched her face. "I did it because I believe that you have talent, no—more than talent, a gift for revealing truth through your acting. That's rare enough to be very special, Sasha. You deserve to be an actress. You deserve to be a star if that's what you want."

The simplicity of his answer brought tears to her eyes. With so few words he had told her everything she needed to know about him. He could give and give generously, even at huge cost to himself. His expression told her he wanted to share it all with her, everything he had to give— the newborn love in his heart, the passion in his loins, the future children in his seed.

"Yes," she said.

"Yes what? You want to be a star?"

Laughing and crying at the beautiful concern in his eyes, she was amazed that he didn't know what she meant. "Yes, I will marry you."

THE EDITOR'S CORNER

This coming month brings to mind lions and lambs—not only in terms of the weather, but also in terms of our six delightful LOVESWEPTs. You'll find fierce and feisty, tame and gentle characters in our books next month who add up to a rich and exciting array of folks whose stories of falling in love are enthralling.

First, hold on to your hat as a really hot wind blows through chilly London town in Fayrene Preston's marvelous *The Pearls of Sharah II: RAINE'S STORY*, LOVESWEPT #318. When Raine Bennett realized someone was following her through foggy Hyde Park one night, she ran . . . straight into the arms of Michael Carr. He was a stranger who radiated danger and mystery—yet he was a man Raine instinctively knew she could trust. Michael was utterly captivated by her, but the magnificent strand of perfect pearls draped across her exquisite body complicated things. What was she doing with the legendary Pearls of Sharah, which had just been reported stolen to his branch of Interpol? What were her secrets and would she threaten his integrity . . . as well as his heart? This is a dazzling love story you just can't let yourself miss! (Do remember that the Doubleday hardcover edition is available at the same time the paperback is in the stores. Don't miss this chance to collect all three Pearls of Sharah romances in these beautifully bound editions at only $12.95.)

Jan Hudson's **THE RIGHT MOVES**, LOVESWEPT #319, will set your senses ablaze. Jan created two unique characters in her heroine and hero; they were yin and yang, fire and ice, and they could not stay away from each other no matter how hard they tried. Chris Ponder was a spitfire, a dynamo with a temper . . . and with a tow truck. When she took one look at Nick Russo's bedroom eyes, her insides turned to tapioca, and she suddenly wanted to flirt with the danger he represented. But good sense started to prevail. After all, she hardly needed to fall for a handsome charmer who might be all flash and no substance. Still Nick teased, and she felt she might go up in flames . . . especially on one moonlit night that filled her with wonder. This is a breathlessly exciting romance!

In LOVESWEPT #320, **THE SILVER BULLET AFFAIR**, Sandra Chastain shows us once again that love sure can conquer all. When John Garmon learned that his brother Jeffrey's will instructed him to "Take care of Caitlan and the

(continued)

baby—it's mine," he immediately sought out the quicksilver lady who had charmed him at every former meeting. Caitlan proved to be like a fine perfume—good at disappearing and very elusive. She believed that John was her adversary, a villain, perhaps, who might take her baby away if he learned the truth. So how could she lose herself in the hot shivery sensations of his embrace? Bewitched by this fragile woman who broke all the rules, John grows determined to rescue Caitlan from her free-spirited life and the gang of crazy but caring friends who never leave them alone to learn to love each other. A shimmering, vivid love story that we think you'll find a real delight.

The brilliant . . . fun . . . thrilling . . . surprising conclusion to the "Hagen Strikes Again" series, by Kay Hooper, **ACES HIGH**, LOVESWEPT #321, comes your way next month. Skye Prescott was tall, dark, and dangerous, a man who'd never forgotten how Katrina Keller had betrayed him years before. In a world where survival depended on suspicion, he'd fallen in love—and it had broken him as violence never had. When the beautiful redheaded ghost from his past reappeared in his life, Skye was filled with fury, hurt, a desire for revenge—and an aching hunger to make Katrina burn for him again. Katrina had fought her memories, but once she was in his arms, she couldn't fight him or her own primal passion. She was his match, his mate—but belonging to him body and spirit gave him the power to destroy her. When Skye faced his most violent enemy, Trina knew she faced the most desperate gamble of her life. Now, friends, need I tease you with the fact that Hagen also gets his in this fabulous book? I know you've been wondering (as all of us here have) what Kay was going to do for that paunchy devil in terms of a love story. Well, next month you will know. And I can guarantee that Kay has been as delightfully inventive as we had hoped and dreamed she would be.

Please give a great, warm welcome to talented new author Marcia Evanick by getting and enjoying her powerfully emotional romance, **PERFECT MORNING**, LOVESWEPT #322. How this story will touch your heart! When Jason Nesbit entered Riki McCormick's front yard in search of his young daughter, he never expected to find an emerald-eyed vixen as her foster mother. He had just learned that he had a child when his ex-wife died in an accident. Traumatized after her mother's death, the girl had not spoken since. Jason marveled at Riki's houseful of love—and was capti-

(continued)

vated by the sweet, spirited woman who'd made room in her life for so many special children. Under Jason's steamy scrutiny, Riki felt a wave of longing to be kissed breathless and held tight. When his Texas drawl warned her that her waiting days were over, she unpacked her slinkiest lingerie and dreamed of satin sheets and firelight. But courting Riki with seven children around seemed downright impossible. You'll laugh and cry with Jason and Riki as they try to make everyone happy. A keeper!

Halsey Morgan is alive—and Stevie Lee wanted him dead. What a way to open a romance! Glenna McReynolds has created two wonderful, thrilling characters in LOVESWEPT #323, **STEVIE LEE.** Halsey Morgan was Stevie Lee's long-lost neighbor. She had plotted for the last few years to buy his cabin for his back taxes, sell it for a huge profit, and get out of her small town so she could see the world. Handsome Halsey had blazed a trail of adventure from the Himalayas to the Amazon—and was thought to be dead. Now he was back—ruining her plans to escape and melting her with sizzling kisses that almost made her forget why she'd ever wanted to go away. His wildness excited her senses to riot, while his husky voice made her tremble with want. Hal had never stayed anywhere long enough to fall in love, but Stevie was the answer to a loneliness he'd never dared admit. He made her take chances, climb mountains, and taught her how to love him. But could Hal persuade her to risk loving him and follow her dreams while held tight in his arms? Don't miss this great story . . . which, we think you'll agree, knocks your socks off!

Enjoy those blustery days next month curled up with six LOVESWEPTs that are as hot as they are happily-ever-after.

Carolyn Nichols

Carolyn Nichols
Editor
LOVESWEPT
Bantam Books
666 Fifth Avenue
New York, NY 10103